J. Fredk. Smith

Gustavus Vasa

Or King and Peasant

J. Fredk. Smith

Gustavus Vasa
Or King and Peasant

ISBN/EAN: 9783743479210

Manufactured in Europe, USA, Canada, Australia, Japa

Cover: Foto ©Raphael Reischuk / pixelio.de

Manufactured and distributed by brebook publishing software (www.brebook.com)

J. Fredk. Smith

Gustavus Vasa

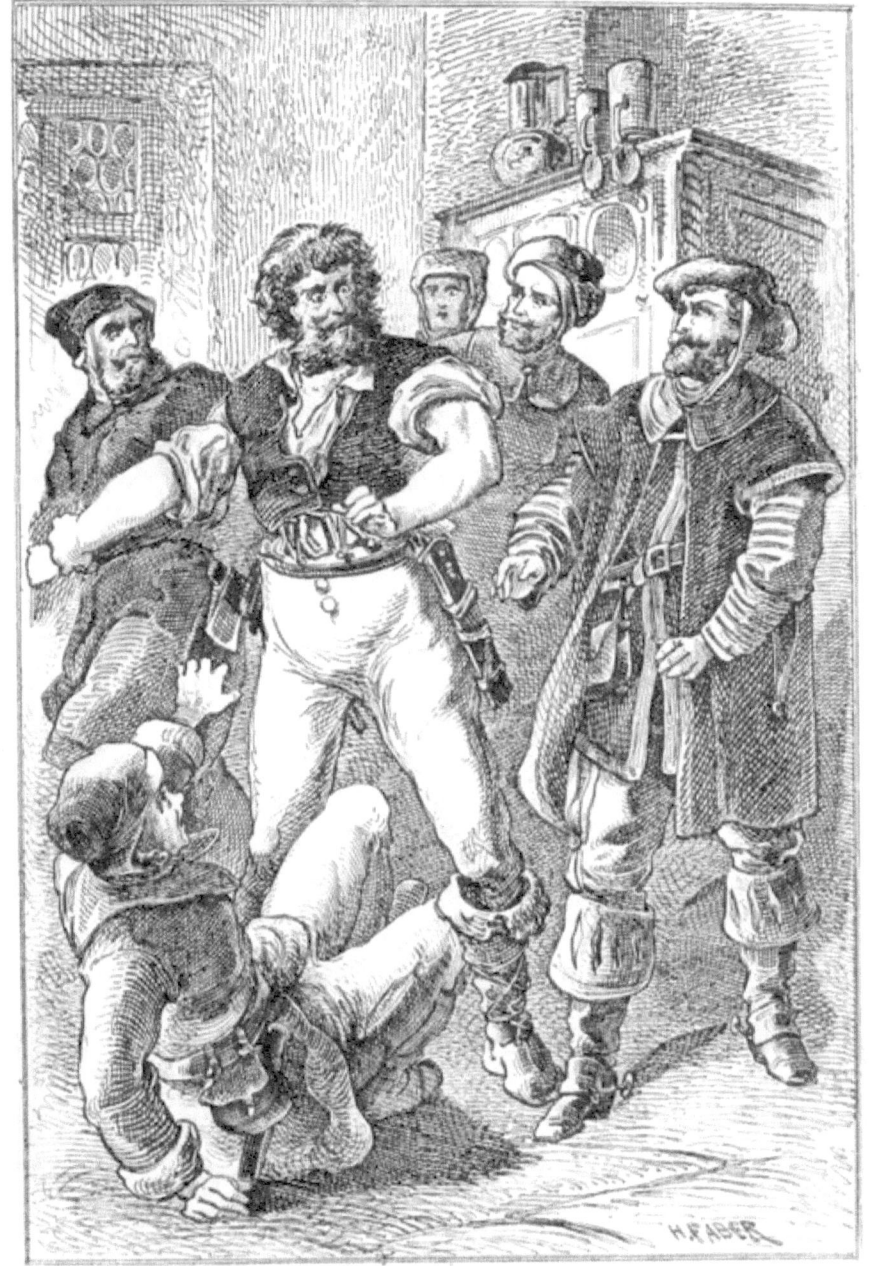

Gustavus Vasa;

OR,

KING AND PEASANT.

From the German of Gustab Nieritz.

BY

J. FREDK. SMITH.

WITH A HISTORIC SKETCH AND NOTES, BY

REV. PROF. A. L. GUSS, A.M.

PHILADELPHIA:
LUTHERAN BOARD OF PUBLICATION,
42 NORTH NINTH ST.
1872.

STEREOTYPED BY J. FAGAN & SON, PHILADELPHIA.

CAXTON PRESS OF SHERMAN & CO.

PUBLISHED

BY

REV. PROF. A. L. GUSS,

PRINCIPAL OF THE SOLDIERS' ORPHANS' SCHOOL,

CASSVILLE, HUNTINGDON CO.,

PENNSYLVANIA.

CONTENTS

GUSTAVUS VASA.

CHAPTER I.

A SILLY PEASANT.

HISTORY is not written merely for our amusement. It is rather a mirror which shows us what we should, or should not, be; how we should, or should not, act. It is, at the same time, a judge,—an incorruptible judge, and no respecter of persons, —a judge whose sentences are not buried among dust-covered statutes, but are open to the inspection of the world. Those children of men, however, who will suffer no other arbiter over them, and who are wont to consider themselves above the laws, espe-

ones. On the contrary, the man with the red hair, who lay in the tallest and softest grass, with his face turned down, was one of the best-fed, stoutest, and tallest of mortals. Three shepherd boys, whose flocks of sheep were scattered over the distant hills, were amusing themselves by cutting branches off the willows, and making them into rude fifes. One of the cows, also, happened to stick her head between the willow-bushes; not, indeed, with any notion of imitating the boys, but that she might taste, for once, something different from her ordinary food; for, even among animals, there are occasionally dainty mouths that long for a taste of something new.

As one of the boys turned round to look at the four-footed gourmand, he exclaimed: "There lies the big, lazy Bav, pressing the grass to the ground with his huge paunch. He has milked the cows, and let all the milk run into his monstrous mouth. This hard work has made him tired, and now he lies there fast asleep, while his sister-in-law wonders why the cows give so little milk, and why they do not grow fat. A pretty herdsman! He cares not whether the wolf comes and tears the cows, or whether they fall into the lake."

"I'll drive the red-haired monster into the water," exclaimed the second boy, "till his limbs are tired out."

"You?" laughed the third. "How can you drive him into the lake?"

"Will you bet?"—betting is the first and last resort of uneducated minds—"I'll bet as much of anything as you like, Malo! But you must help me," returned the boy. "Here's my fife for a wager—stake yours against it; and you do the same with yours, Levin!"

The bet was taken.

2

Thereupon Tauwson cried out, " Malo, you drive the cows into the thicket; and you, Levin, make haste and throw this old willow-knot into the lake."

While the two boys were executing these orders, Tauwson ran to the sleeper, seized a ram's horn lying by his side, put it to his mouth, and, bending down to Bav's left ear, gave a blast so loud and piercing that one would have expected it to crack the tym-panum of any ordinary person.

Any other man would have started, fright-ened at the sound; but Bav's dull nature comprehended only enough to cause him to raise his head and stare stupidly at Tauw-son.

" Bav! Bav!" cried Tauwson. "A wolf! Bav! a wolf!"

" W-h-e-r-e?" asked the giant, slowly.

" Think you he'll wait for your heavy club, you foolish Bav?" answered Tauwson. "He has already torn to pieces one of the cows, and the others he has driven into the lake. For shame, Bav! See, brown Rieke still holds her head above the water yonder! Make haste, if you would save her. Ha! what will your sister-in-law say to this; and how will your insatiable stomach fare, too, when it can no longer have plenty of milk?"

The latter suggestion. may have had the greater effect upon Bav. He sprang up, ran to the lake, looked at the floating willow-knot, which, indeed, was not unlike a horned cow's head, and then plunged quickly into the water, striking out vigorously with his sturdy arms.

"The fifes are mine!" cried Tauwson, triumphantly. "I've won the bet. There swims the silly Bav like a duck. See, he has just discovered the trick. It's lucky I am not the willow-knot, or I'd pay dearly for my fun. How savagely he snorts."

" He 's nearing the shore," observed Malo, anxiously. " Listen how he groans with rage. Take to your heels, Tauwson, or you are lost ! "

Before the giant reached the shore, the three boys had wisely run away. Bav stood still for a second, sputtering, and shaking himself like an angry bear; then he picked up a heavy stone and threw it with all his might after the fleeing trio. Had the stone not missed its aim, it would surely have killed one of his tormentors. He then started to run after them ; but his steps became shorter and shorter the nearer he approached his old resting-place. Bav's inherent laziness overcame his thirst for revenge. A satisfied look at the seven cows now coming out of the willow-copse, a few unintelligible threats, and Bav again laid himself down in the tall grass, leaving to the sun the easy task of drying his clothes.

The three boys halted upon the hill on which their sheep were grazing, whence they watched Bav's actions, or rather his indolence.

"He's not pretending," said Levin, "in order to entice us to him; he's really asleep."

"Whoever hits the lazy giant with his sling, at the third throw, shall receive his fife back again," proposed Tauwson, with his usual propensity for betting.

Throwing with the sling, in which they all took part, now began, and lasted some time; but not one of the many stones had yet hit the sleeper. The boys grew more and more excited, and did not notice who it was that now stepped among them with the question: "What are you aiming at, boys?"

"Hah! Henrik! is it you?" exclaimed Malo, delighted. "It's your silly uncle's back we are aiming at. Instead of minding the cows, the lazy idler is lying yonder in the grass."

"Are you throwing stones at him?" re-turned the boy, angrily. "I won't suffer that."

"Oh!" returned Levin, apologetically, "we have not struck him once yet; and, besides, Bav has a skin as tough as an old bull's. I doubt if he would get awake if even one of the stones should hit him."

"Well, we will see," said Henrik; "but you stop throwing. I'll try to wake my lazy uncle with one of these beautiful red apples in my pocket."

With these words, Henrik unbuttoned his sling, and put an apple into the loop. He then prepared to throw, first measuring with his eye the distance from him to Bav. The other boys, notwithstanding Henrik was known to be a very expert slinger, followed his motions with incredulous smiles.

Henrik swung the sling quicker and quicker till suddenly he let go one end of it, and the

apple sped through the air. Describing a wide
circle, it descended towards the ground.

That instant Bav sprang up from the grass
with a roar of pain. Tauwson, Malo, and
Levin hid, in alarm, among the sheep. Bav
bellowed terribly. He rubbed the back of his
head with his hand, and looked about for his
enemies. Seeing no one but his nephew, who
was coming rapidly towards him, he sprang
away, howling with pain and rage, and in a
little while was out of sight.

"There!" said Henrik to the boys; "if,
instead of the apple, one of these stones had
struck my uncle's head, he would not have
sprung up and run away."

A long conversation between the boys now
followed, during which Henrik learned that
his uncle had, as usual, milked the cows, after
which he had taken no further interest in
them, and that he had gotten a cold bath into
the bargain. The boys turned round in sur-

prise as they heard behind them the well-known voice of the pastor of Swärdsiö, who thus addressed them : " What ails poor Bav, who is running towards the village bawling and howling ? He refused even to speak to me."

The boys, conscious of their guilt, were at first silent from shame. At last, however, they answered, confessing their fault to their pastor, who reproved them earnestly.

" Perhaps, foolish boys," he said, " you hope, by such conduct, to improve Bav's laziness ? But you will only make him wicked and revengeful. He might then, in his blind fury, destroy the innocent ; — yes, the whole village might suffer. Alas ! the poor fellow is so unfortunate already, and is so unfitted for the enjoyment of life ; why do you thus aggravate his wretchedness by your thoughtless injuries ? Believe me, boys, kind treatment and instruction would make him much more intelligent and tractable. And you, Henrik, Bav's own nephew, how can *you* treat him thus? Oh, fie! what a sin!"

"My dear pastor," returned the youth, with tears in his eyes, "Bav is our constant torment. Not a day passes that my mother does not have to weep because of him. He eats and drinks as much as five servants, and does not work half as hard as a servant does. And, besides, he's so awkward that he ruins everything he handles. We often go hungry because he consumes the whole meal himself. Only last evening mother caught him emptying the cheese-basket, and greedily swallowing the cheese. We can keep nothing from him; for he is so strong that he can burst open all the doors, or lift them off their hinges. Instead of watching our cows, he secretly milks them, and drinks all the milk. Only look how thin the poor creatures are!"

"It is, indeed, a great misfortune," replied

the pastor, "but you dare not forget that Bav
is your sainted father's only brother.   Bear
with his infirmities, and God will surely bless
you for it in some way that seems good to
Him."

With these words, the good pastor departed on his round through his extensive
parish.

CHAPTER II.

THE CANNIBAL.

BAV sat in the family room of his sister-in-law, leaning his head upon the well-scoured table, weeping bitterly. No one else was there; for Fru Mindson, with all her servants and children, was at work in the field. Rosanna, her oldest daughter, a girl of thirteen, was busy cleaning and putting in order the kitchen. When she returned, in a little while, to the sitting-room, and found Bav there sobbing so violently, she said to him, reproachfully and yet gently: "Bav, have you been doing some silly thing again? Oh, Bav! you are our uncle; but say, how can we respect you, when you thus commit one foolish act after another, and give our mother so much trouble and anxiety? Uncle, what have you been doing now?"

At these words Bav raised his head, and let his niece look into a pair of large blue eyes, swimming in tears. It was a touching sight, to see this gigantic man weeping and sobbing like a child. After looking at his niece a while in silence, he again laid his head upon the table.

"Your clothes are dripping wet, and are all muddy," continued Rosanna; "did you fall into the lake, Bav?"

Here Bav's sobbing changed into a fierce howl.

"Do answer me, Bav?" urged Rosanna, laying her hand on her uncle's wet hair. She withdrew it quickly, in an alarmed manner, exclaiming: "Dear me! what a lump: what has happened, Bav?"

With a whine, which was not unlike the roar of a lion, Bav cried: "Henrik — with a sling! Oh! oh!" and he pressed his hand upon the wound, and wept still more bitterly.

"I would not have thought this of the wicked fellow," said Rosanna, indignantly. "But he shall be punished for it as soon as mother returns from the field."

While Rosanna was preparing a cold-water poultice for her uncle's wound, she said, half-aloud, "I only wonder that the big Bav did not kill the boys in his anger. Ah, Bav!" she continued, in a louder tone; "if only you were not so greedy, so dainty-mouthed, so lazy and silly. Just think of the basket of cheese yesterday. And early this morning, although you had already swallowed a larger plate of soup than both the servants had eaten, did you not empty two bowls full of milk; and, in doing so, did you not overturn two others with your foot, and spill ever so much milk in the cellar? And, two hours after, did you not suck the eleven eggs which,

3

a little while before, we had put under the old hen? And just after dinner, did you not steal from the oven a large loaf of bread? And did you not empty into the pond the bag of rye, which you were too lazy to carry to the mill? Who can count the sausages and hams which have disappeared from the chimney and have wandered into your rapacious maw? Can you deny it, Bav?"

Bav was silent, thus confessing his guilt.

"We are orphans," continued Rosanna, "and instead of having a father in you, who should be an example to the servants and maids, you are more destructive than any of them. You will make us poor yet — no, we have become poor already because of you. Our mother is not able to pay the taxes; and when the collector comes to demand his money, she will have to sell one of the cows. She has spoken of this already, and has selected brown Rieke as the one to be sold."

"Brown Rieke?" cried Bav. "I won't suffer that. If the collector comes, I'll kill him."

"You dare not do so," reasoned Rosanna; "for the King sends him, and what the King commands, that we must do. He does not wear the sword in vain; and already has he caused many a one, who did not do his will, to feel it."

"Not brown Rieke?" repeated Bav, stubbornly. "I will not suffer it." And he struck his fist so violently upon the table that the well-worn piece of furniture broke, and fell with a crash to the floor.

"Is it any fault of mine that everything breaks to pieces beneath my hands and feet?" cried Bav, angrily.

"Go to Falun," urged Rosanna, "and try your strength upon the hard rock in the copper-mines; or become a wood-cutter; or go into the cities and harbors, where porters

and carriers are needed.   You are of no manner of use here.   The dead water, that has
neither arms nor legs, is more industrious
than you, for at least it turns the mill-wheel.
Now just look at our serviceable table!   If
only Henrik would come soon and glue it
together before mother sees it, and vexes herself anew."

"Rosanna!" said Bav, confidentially, "you
are the best among them all.   Say, what
shall I do?   I will follow your advice; but
must I not eat when I am hungry?   And I
am hungry and thirsty all the time!"

"It's nothing but a foolish habit, Bav," returned Rosanna.   "By your incessant eating
and drinking, you have created an unnatural
appetite, and distended your stomach.   Your
voracious, craving appetite is by no means
natural hunger.   If the blow on your head
had only made you sensible!   Indeed, I have
heard of the like, and heartily wish it had

knocked good sense into your head. Oh, Bav! if you were only rational!"

"I will be!" asserted Bav, half weeping, half laughing. "How shall I begin? What must I do?"

"Go, first, and bring Henrik," answered Rosanna; "we will then talk about it further."

Bav ran out of the room.

"If he were to become rational," repeated Rosanna, as she went to look for the glue-pot, "how glad mother would be. But the table! the table! I wonder whether the glue will hold so that I can ever scour it again with warm water!"

Rosanna's attention was now attracted to a carriage that stopped before the door, from which alighted a well-dressed woman and her two little boys.

"A hearty welcome, Fru Ribbing," said Rosanna, as she hastily approached the vis-

3 *_

itor, and extended her hand to her and the children. " You wish to see my mother ? "

" Yes," replied Fru Ribbing. " It occurred to me, while riding by, that your mother lately told me that she intended to sell one of her cows. If she is of the same mind still, and I like the animal, we can no doubt strike a bargain."

" 'T is well that Bav is not here," said Rosanna to herself, and then replied, aloud, " Mother is out in the field. Have patience a little while, and I 'll bring her, and the cows too that are grazing in the meadow."

" No, my child," said Fru Ribbing; "towards evening I will return through your village; it will then be a more suitable time to speak to your mother, and to look at the cows. But do you not see, Rosanna, how much my two boys have grown since last you saw them ? "

As she asked the question, Fru Ribbing

looked with motherly tenderness upon her handsome, stout-looking boys, whose flaxen locks she stroked by turns. "They have on to-day, for the first time, their new blue velvet jackets," she continued. "But they have faithfully promised me to take good care of them. Frederick, take your handkerchief and brush off the stool before you sit down. It is scoured very clean, but yet there may be some grains of sand upon it, which would soon rub the gloss off your fine jacket. They are good boys, Rosanna, — but I should not praise them to their faces. Frederick will be seven years old next St. Martin's day, and Armfred will be five years of age by Candlemas. See, Rosanna, do not the pretty white neckties contrast beautifully with the blue velvet? and the golden locks, which curl so naturally, are they not very becoming? Ha, Frederick, you little rogue! why are you looking at me so innocently with your honest

blue eyes? I shall leave you for a few moments with Rosanna, while I look around the
yard and into the stable; for we can always
learn something useful, even in our old age:
albeit I am not yet old. Meantime, Rosanna
will tell you a pretty story, or amuse you in
some other way."

Fru Ribbing then left the house, not, however, without stopping in the doorway and
calling back: "Armfred! Frederick! be careful of your pretty jackets."

Rosanna remained behind in some embarrassment, from which the older of the two
boys soon relieved her by asking, as he
pointed to the table, " Did the cannibal do
this ? "

" What cannibal ? " answered Rosanna, in
astonishment.

" The one our Morija told us about. Do
you not know the pretty story ? "

" No, Frederick: won't you tell it to me ? "

" Once upon a time," the little fellow began,
"there was a cannibal, who was as tall as a
church-steeple, and had fingers as long and
as thick as the largest sausages. He had
fiery-red hair, and he carried in his hand a
huge fir-tree as a staff. When he was thirsty,
he drank dry a little brook; and it was no
great labor for him to devour a whole herd
of sheep, skins and all. Now, one day the
cannibal returned home carrying a man on
his shoulder, just as if he was a feather. His
wife, who also was a giant, but not so cruel
as her husband, took the man and carried
him into the kitchen. Half an hour later,
the husband bawled out, 'Wife! I'm hungry;
bring me some supper!' The wife obeyed,
and prepared to set a number of dishes upon
the table, which was as large as a barn-door.
There was an ox roasted whole, ten sheep,
three pigs, five calves, and, besides these, a
big bowl of mush, and a huge pile of loaves

of bread as large as wagon-wheels. And yet this cannibal was not satisfied. He smelled every dish with his tremendous nose, making a noise like a smith's bellows, and said, 'I smell no human flesh! Where have you put the fellow I brought in?' Then his wife, all of-a-tremble, answered, 'Indeed, my dear husband, I have not had time to roast him. You would not wait any longer; and, besides, he wept so bitterly, and lamented so for his wife and children. He begged me only to let him live till to-morrow.' 'No!' grumbled the angry cannibal, 'I'll eat him to-day,—this very minute!' And with this he struck so hard upon the table that he broke it; and as it fell, all that was upon it tumbled on the cannibal's legs, which were stretched out beneath it. Ha! ha! ha!"

"Ha! ha! ha!" laughed little Armfred also. " It served him right."

"Yes," answered Frederick, " it served the

cannibal just right. Why did he wish to eat up, the poor man? Well, the hot roast burned the cannibal's legs so severely that he could never stand on his feet again, and mortification soon set in. Then, too, in the corner of the table there had been a large nail, the point of which stuck out a great way. This the cannibal had struck with his fist, making a great hole in his hand, and soon his whole arm became swollen. There lay the big giant till he died, unable to move a limb for three long days. And his wife was frightened so much that she forgot all about the man, who luckily managed to run away. Now, Rosanna, was it not he who broke *your* table?"

"There comes the cannibal!" suddenly exclaimed little Armfred, as tremblingly he crept behind his older brother, whose words died upon his lips. He stared, pale as death, at the door, in which appeared a — giant.

Bav, the giant Bav, entered the room. He carried, over his shoulder, his nephew Henrik, whom he now lifted down with wonderful ease. Then he brushed the hair from his face with his broad hand, and, panting like the blowing of a huge bellows, he cried in a loud voice to Rosanna, "Here's the fellow! Have you put the glue-pot on the fire?"

At this the two boys now screamed so loudly that the noise soon brought the mother into the room. Frederick and Armfred, still shrieking, ran to her and hid their faces in the folds of her dress. The rest looked on in astonishment. She, however, recognized at once in Bav the cause of their fright, and said to Rosanna, hurriedly, "Greet your mother for me. Frederick! Armfred! do be quiet! Tell your mother that this evening — for shame, boys! the man will not hurt you; he is Rosanna's uncle."

Feeble as was the mind of Bav, he yet comprehended that he was the cause of the boys' fright, and, as was natural with one of his disposition, a strong dislike. for the boys came over him, which he expressed by fierce looks and gestures; and when Fru Ribbing let fall some words about buying the cow, his ill-humor increased beyond measure. " No cows must be sold," he cried, in a threatening voice; "brown Rieke must stay here. I 'll kill any one that comes to take her away ! " To add strength to his words, he struck once more with his fist upon the table, whose joints cracked beneath the powerful blow.

Fru Ribbing, frightened almost as much as were her children, ran off with her little ones, never again to cross Fru Mindson's threshold.

This much at least had Bav effected by his outburst of rage.

What a fright to others, and what a torment to himself, is the person who cannot govern

4

his temper. Self-discipline is, indeed, the true end of all intellectual exertion; for " he that ruleth his own spirit is greater than he that taketh a city." Poor Bav was not greatly worse than many of sounder mind.

CHAPTER III.

THE AWKWARD THRASHER.

THE town of Falun, in Sweden, has for centuries been noted for its copper mines. The mine, which opens in the centre of the great market square of the town, occupies a great deal of room, and reveals to the spectator a deep pit, swarming with busy workmen. Here, one October day in the year 1520, stood Bav Mindson, striking with hammer and pick upon the hard rock. With a dingy, black, miner's cap stuck upon his shock of red hair, and his huge form clad in the customary miner's dress, which was covered over partly with reddish-brown earth, partly with copper-green paint, he presented an unsightly appearance. He looked down

before him, with eyebrows knit ominously
together. His once full, red cheeks hung
pale and lank, and it could easily be seen
that it was with great difficulty he performed
his work. In a little while he stopped, sighed
heavily, and looked gloomily around. Then
he became absorbed in thought,—if we can
speak thus of such a dull creature,— and remained for a time inactive, till a voice cried
to him: "You must work harder, Mindson.
You have filled very few boxes with ore to-
day, and will receive but scanty wages; you
will then suffer hunger."

Hunger! The terrible word had its effect
on Bav. The recollection of hunger seemed
to arouse within him hunger itself, which, fortunately for him, till now had slumbered. He
was suddenly seized with a ravenous appetite,
to satisfy which he, alas! had no means. For
to-day, soon after breakfast, he had eaten the
food that had been intended for his dinner.

Half unconsciously, he laid his covetous hand upon his neighbor's parcel,—which, doubtless, was as tempting to him as was the apple to Eve in Paradise. Before the miner could demand the restoration of his property, Bav had opened the bundle and taken a huge bite from the loaf of black bread.

" Thief! " cried the miner to Bav. " Wait a bit; I 'll tell this to the overseer. He will deduct the value of my bread from your day's wages; and he 'll turn you off besides, for we 'll have nothing to do with thieves here."

" Take the bread from the rascal, Peterson! " exclaimed an angry workman. " Pay him what he deserves."

" I 'd only repent of it if I did," returned Peterson. " Have you forgotten already, Heinke, that the silly Bav whipped six strong men, who were amusing themselves at his expense? No, no; sound limbs are worth more than a piece of bread, say I."

4 *

"It tastes bitter!" grumbled Bav, eating the while.

"I only wish," said Peterson, "it would turn to verdigris in your ugly mouth."

"Everything tastes bitter here," continued Bav, in a melancholy tone. "And no meat, and no eggs, and no bacon. Oh!" he sighed, "and no Rosanna to comfort me."

Weeping bitterly, Bav continued eating his bread, while the big tears rolled down his sunken cheeks.

"Give the thief a blow on the head, Peterson," cried Heinke again; and as his suggestion was unheeded, he seized a piece of ore, and threw it with a sure aim at Bav's shaggy head.

Bav opened wide his huge mouth and uttered a fearful yell; at the same instant he let fall his hammer and pick, and held his wounded head with both hands. In wild, blind rage, he hastened from the mine, running with his body bent almost double, shoving aside everything that stood in his way; and climbing, screaming all the while, to the top of the mine, deigning no explanation to the other miners, nor heeding in the least their calls.

On he ran for almost an hour, till he reached the parish of Wika, and in it the house of his master, the rich proprietor, Wjarren.

"What do you want, Mindson?" the master asked, astonished at seeing his miner return home at so unusual an hour.

"My head!" answered Bav, in broken accents. "I'll work there no more. Everything tastes bitter there."

"You foolish fellow," laughed Wjarren. "After you have become used to the copper taste nothing will taste bitter to you. Did you not promise me, inasmuch as you eat so much, to do the work of four men? Have

you abandoned your good intention already?
What can I do with you if you will not
work in the mine?"

"I'll work there no more," protested Bav,
stubbornly.

"Then you must help thrash a while," said
Wjarren, after a little reflection. "Ha!
Anke, show the fellow to the barn, where
you two can help Wason thrash the rye. In
the evening, when the other miners return,
they shall tell me why Mindson has run
away."

The maid Anke did not view the new
thrasher with much favor, notwithstanding
his fingers might almost be compared to
flails, and she grumbled to herself, "*He'll*
make a fine thrasher. The one is just as
stupid as the other. I may consider myself
fortunate if I get away with a whole head."

The thrashing began; not, however, in the
usual measured manner, but irregularly, and

with frequent interruptions. It was easy to
know when Bav struck with his flail, for the
whole barn shook with every blow. In a
little while, when Wjarren came to look on,
the girl ran to him, her face flushed with
anger.

"Some one else must do this work," she
said to her master. "Mindson has already
the fifth flail in his hands. The first four are
lying broken around the barn. If luckily I
escape a blow from Mindson, the equally
awkward Wason strikes me on the ear. It's
a wonder I 've not been killed. There! *that 's*
Mindson. He drives a sheaf into the floor
with every blow, so that the grain and straw
are mixed with the clay." While Anke was
yet speaking, there was heard a terrible crash,
produced by one of the flails striking against
the wooden barn-door. Bav, the awkward
fellow, who could eat bread, but could not
thrash out the grain necessary to make it, had

struck himself on the head with his flail, and had thrown it from him in his rage. On entering the barn, Wjarren found his two thrashers in nearly similar attitudes, each holding his bruised head. At the sight of his master, Wason at once removed his hand from his wound, and endeavored to suppress any exclamation of pain; but he could not conceal the great lump on his head.

Wjarren cast a hasty glance at the howling Bav, and then, turning to Wason, asked, " Is this the first time in your life, Wason, that you have tried to swing the flail?"

"Why do you ask?" returned Wason, not altogether without embarrassment.

"Because of this proof," answered Wjarren, pointing to the lump on Wason's forehead.

"This would have happened to the most expert of thrashers," replied Wason, "had he been placed opposite this clumsy Mindson."

"I take you at your word, Wason!" said Wjarren; "take your flail: I will help you instead of Mindson. Come, Anke!"

"Pardon me, Herre, for declining the honor," said Wason. "The blow on my forehead has quite stunned me; I can scarcely stand."

At this unusual reply from a common laborer, Wjarren looked at the young man with a suspicious shrug of the shoulder, which made Wason blush. Anke, the maid, made mysterious signs to her master; but he did not understand the gestures, and, addressing Bav, he gave him his choice, either to return to the mine, or leave his service, to which Bav replied with only an angry growl.

In the evening, when the servants, the maids, and the miners were together at meal-time, there was lively chatting and jesting. There were but two who did not join therein, Wason and Bav, who sat quiet and absorbed, although the latter forgot not to satisfy his ravenous appetite. It would be his last meal here, for he had most decidedly refused to return to the mine. All the more frugal was Wason, who left the room even before the meal was ended, saying that his head pained him greatly. He had scarcely gone, when the conversation was directed to the mysterious stranger.

" This Wason is just as much a real peasant as I am a baron," said one. " I believe he knows better how to wield the sword than the flail."

" And he sits upon a horse like any nobleman," asserted another, " even when he is mounted on an old farm-horse."

" Does he ever join with us in saying our accustomed grace, which any child knows by heart?" asked a servant-maid. " Even this shows that he is no common man."

" And his manner of speaking," began

another; "is it not high-sounding, even when he tries to speak as we do?"

"Only look at his hands," said a third; "how white and soft they are! Who of us can boast of such a skin as Wason has?"

"And does he take any part in our jests and merry sports?" asked a miner. "Does he not always quietly withdraw from among us, and go away alone?"

"Yes," said another, "and whither? To the hollow willow by the lake, where I saw, at a distance, how he drew from it a handsome suit, and quickly concealed it again when he got a sight of me. I searched the willow afterwards, but the bird had emptied its nest, and carried the eggs elsewhere."

"*He's a* SWEDE," suggested another, "and not a Dane. This accounts for his mysterious behavior. King Christian has not many friends in Sweden, and who knows—"

"You know nothing about it, Dricks!"

interrupted Anke; "but I discovered something to-day that's better than all your
guesses. I noticed it while thrashing with
Wason and Mindson."

"What! Anke! Speak!" was the exclamation of all.

"That you may tell our master before me,
and claim the honor of the discovery," returned Anke. "The master did not understand my signs to him, else he would have
seen it with his own eyes. You shall hear
of it to-morrow."

As the girl was firm in her determination,
and proved deaf to all their eager questions,
the curious miners endeavored to learn
something from Bav; but their efforts were
fruitless. The unobservant Bav had noticed
nothing, and knew nothing.

The following morning, after the miners
had gone to their work, and the laborers to
the field, Wjarren called into his room the

man Wason, whom he had purposely de-
tained.   As he entered the room, Wjarren
looked him steadily in the face.

"Wason," began the proprietor, "if you
are an honest Swede, answer me candidly
and unreservedly.   Why do you disguise
yourself as a common servant, which you
are not?"

"Why do you think so, Herre?" answered
Wason, composedly.

"My good eyes, and those of my people,
tell me that I am right," replied Wjarren.
"As you value your safety, tell me the truth."

"I am truly a Swede, and a friend of my
country," confessed Wason, "and not a servant born."

"And is this all you have to make known
to me?" asked Wjarren, sternly; and step-
ping close up to Wason, he unbuttoned his
doublet to the neck.   "Yesterday you wore
beneath your doublet a gold-stitched collar;

why do you not have it on to-day? Shall I
summon Anke as a witness? You dare not
consent to face the proof. I ask you again:
who are you, and why do you disguise yourself?"

"Has the pursuit of earthly mammon so
blinded *you*, or has grief for my Fatherland so
changed *me*," said Wason, in a voice full of
emotion, "that you cannot recognize in me a
former University friend? Why look at me
in such amazement? Must I inform you
that I am GUSTAVUS ERIKSON, of the House
of Vasa, with whom you studied ten years
ago, in Upsala?"

Wjarren turned pale. "You Gustavus
Erikson?" he stammered. "How did you
return to Sweden, having been sent as a
hostage to King Christian?"

"Are you the only man in Sweden," asked
Wason, indignantly, "who knows not how
treacherously King Christian has trodden

under foot the most sacred law of nations?
Under pretence of desiring to negotiate
terms of peace with Sweden, and of coming
in person to Stockholm for this purpose, the
Danish King demanded hostages for his safety. My country sent them to him, myself
among the number; whereupon the treacherous Christian ordered us to be arrested and
carried to Denmark; and, instead of going
himself to Stockholm, he threatened my
country that he would behead us unless
she complied with his outrageous demands.
Under such circumstances, have I done
wrong in escaping to my Fatherland?"

Wjarren, confused and silent, stared at the
tips of his fingers.

"And what do you purpose doing now?"
he asked, after a pause, during which Gustavus had watched his former friend with
mingled feelings of pain and anger.

"I will travel through my Fatherland,"

5 *

cried Gustavus, with enthusiasm; "will raise my voice throughout her borders, and rouse the people to shake off the yoke of the foreign oppressor. I will not rest till I—"

"In God's name, silence, unhappy man!" interrupted the terrified Wjarren. "Would you destroy yourself and me too? Your tongue utters high treason; I can listen to you no longer."

"*I* ruin you, friend?" asked Gustavus, bitterly. "Far be it from me! Ah! never can *you* become a free man, for about your neck hangs, heavy as lead, a large mine and a great estate, with houses, and barns, and meadows, and fields. All these you might lose, should you revolt from the foreign tyrant."

"Flee hence!" counselled Wjarren, anxiously. "Flee into the mountains, that you may not fall into the hands of the executioner. Take a horse—"

"I understand," returned Gustavus; "you advise me to take one of your horses, so that you can proclaim that your servant Wason has fled like a thief. I will spare you the falsehood, and will escape on foot. Farewell, Wjarren; and be happy, if happy you *can* be, a slave to King Christian."

Soon after, Gustavus Erikson encountered, in the wood, the dismissed Bav, who was sitting ruefully on a stump, and said to him, in the bitterness of his heart:

"Poor fellow! art thou thinking how thou wilt now satisfy thy voracious stomach? If thou art, I will tell thee how. Become King Christian's executioner, and your troubles will be over."

"Executioner?" said Bav, shaking his head. "Rosanna said nothing about that. 'Go to Falun,' said she, 'into the copper-mines:' and I went. But there everything tasted bitter to me; and then they all made

sport of me, and beat me on the head. It
was all the same with thrashing. O my
poor head! How can I help it that my
stomach craves food and drink all the while?
'Or, go into the cities and harbors,' said
Rosanna, further, 'and be a carrier.' Oh!
Bav does not easily forget anything that
Rosanna says. But by what road can I
reach a harbor? I've been sitting here a
long time trying to find out."

"Thither, Bav!" said Gustavus, not indif-
ferent to the fellow's grief, as he pointed
towards the sea.

Bav thanked him, and left. Gustavus
Vasa looked after him, and murmured,
"Had I but half a thousand as big and as
strong as thou, the faithless Christian should
tremble." With hasty steps he pressed on
into the wood.

CHAPTER IV.

THE BLOODY DEED.

SIX weeks later, Rosanna and Henrik Mindson led brown Rieke, by a rope, out of their mother's farm-yard.

"It's well our Uncle Bav is not here," said the boy: "he would never consent to our leading away brown Rieke."

"I wonder where he can be, poor Bav?" returned Rosanna, sorrowfully. "Since he has gone, no blessing has come upon us. Already we have had to sell a second cow to the butcher in order to pay the taxes! A thousand times have I repented that I advised our uncle to leave us. If only no misfortune has happened to him!"

"Oh!" cried Henrik, "I don't feel wor-

ried about that. Do you not know that fortune ever follows at the heels of a fool?"

Talking thus, the two children left the
yard; their mother gazed after them with
tearful eyes. But not long after, brown
Rieke appeared again in the gateway; this
time led by a much stronger hand, that took
her back into the stall. It was Bav himself,
the big, tall Bav, who now tied brown Rieke
fast in her place, as he pressed his head ca-
ressingly on that of the cow.

"You stay here," said he; "as long as I
am here, no butcher shall dare to harm you.
I have come just in time."

Meantime, Fru Mindson, who was about
to look for her brother-in-law, who had returned so unexpectedly, was met by her
children, who came running to her.

"Oh, mother! mother!" cried Rosanna,
in the greatest glee; "only look how much
silver I've got in my apron!" And she let

the astonished woman look into her gathered apron, from which smiled upon her the tempting glitter of numerous silver coins.

"From Bav!" shouted Rosanna; "from our Bav! He threw the pieces before us by the handful, as if they were miserable pebbles, when I told him we were going to sell brown Rieke because we needed money. Henrik! you have not let any of the dollars lie in the snow?"

"You need n't be afraid of that!" replied Henrik. "I've searched all around, full ten times, where the foolish Bav threw the money."

"How much is there?" asked Fru Mindson, eagerly.

The money was counted,—sixty dollars!

"This will pay the taxes for at least two years!" exclaimed the delighted mother.

"Did I not tell you, 'a fool for luck,'" cried Henrik.

"I wonder how Bav got it?" asked Rosanna, thus rolling a heavy stone upon her mother's heart.

"Yes," said Fru Mindson, suddenly becoming thoughtful; "how could Bav have come by all this money?"

"Ask him," suggested Henrik; "there he comes out of the stable. He does n't look so stout and rosy-cheeked as he used to. Poor fellow! he must have stinted himself a good deal in order to scrape together so much money."

"A hearty welcome, brother-in-law," said Fru Mindson, as she extended to him her hand, in which Bav laid his silently and coldly.

"You have been quite fortunate, I see," continued Fru Mindson.

"Fortunate?" returned Bav, shaking his head. "If any other than you were to say so I 'd break his head."

"Well, you have brought with you a great many bright silver pieces: have you had to work hard for them?" asked the mother, not without anxiety.

Bav looked thoughtfully into the distance, and, after a pause, said, "Work hard? Yes!" he sighed, "hard, very hard!" and he stared upon his emaciated hands.

"You are hungry and thirsty," said Fru Mindson. "I'll go and prepare you a good meal."

"Hungry?" answered Bav. "Did you not say, Rosanna, that hunger was a foolish habit? I have not forgotten it; and I have accustomed myself to hunger. But I thirst all the more. Hand me the pitcher of water, Rosanna."

While Bav was gulping in full draughts, Rosanna whispered anxiously to her mother,

"Oh! dear mother! I cannot like our uncle any more. He used to look at us

6

with his blue eyes so trustingly; and now they wander around so suspiciously and restlessly."

"I beg you, Rosanna," said Fru Mindson, "find out what ails him. You can do more with him than any one else. Speak to him whilst I am preparing something for him to eat."

When Fru Mindson had left the room, Rosanna threw her arms affectionately around Bav's neck, and said to him in flattering tones, "Dear Bav, were you in Falun? Or have you been cutting wood? or did you become a carrier and bear burdens? In what way have you earned so much money?"

Bav sprang up from his seat, raised his shoulders and lifted his arms, as if to adjust a heavy load upon his back; and, as he did so, he murmured, "Bear burdens? Yes, Rosanna, and heavy ones; they weigh upon me yet." And he breathed hard and loud. Then he once more sat down, and unbuttoned his waistcoat so that his shirt could be seen.

"Oh!" cried Rosanna, clasping her hands in terror. "Uncle! your shirt is all bloody!" Then she glanced hastily at Bav's clothing. "Are not these blood-stains also?" she tremblingly inquired, pointing to some spots on his vest.

"And his trowsers look as if they had been dipped in blood!" cried Henrik, who, as Rosanna spoke, observed his uncle more closely.

Bav again rose quickly from his seat. He hastily rebuttoned his waistcoat and hurried to the door, in which his sister-in-law now appeared, her arms well filled with provisions for her relative.

"Whither are you going, Bav?" she asked. "I have brought you food and drink, which

I have prepared as well as I could in such haste."

But Bav, without speaking a word, hastened past her out into the wintry cold.

"What ails him? why does he run away?" cried Fru Mindson, as she looked into the faces of her astonished children.

"Uncle's shirt," stammered Rosanna, "around the collar, was full of blood; and his waistcoat, too, had blood-stains upon it."

"And his trowsers," continued Henrik, "were also bloody. If it is only the blood of an animal, no matter."

"Alas! alas!" exclaimed Fru Mindson, and the provisions fell from her hands; "our uncle! can he have become a robber — a murderer?"

"I cannot believe it," wept Rosanna. "Uncle never was wicked. But the money burns my apron. There, dear mother; take it, take it away!"

"If it should be blood-money?" shuddered the mother. "Henrik! put it in yonder chest."

Henrik, less sensitive than his mother and sister, obeyed; but, in doing so, some of the dollars slipped between his fingers. "Can this be rust or blood that adheres to the bright coins?"

"Are we not more unhappy with all the money," asked the mother, "than we were before? *Ah! of what good are all the treasures of the earth when acquired by dishonest means?*"

Bav did not show himself again all day long.

"His guilt is only too certain," lamented Fru Mindson; "for did any one ever know our Bav to run away when there was anything before him to eat?"

In the evening there arrived at the inn, at Swärdsiö, a traveller, who had come from

Jönköping, whence he had brought exciting and terrible news. As it was noised about, the people of the parish assembled in great numbers, in order to hear the incredible tidings from the mouth of the traveller himself. He was not unwilling to gratify the curiosity of those present, and, surrounded by a dense circle of anxious listeners, he began:

"You already know, my countrymen, that our Fatherland, after a long struggle against Denmark,—not, however, until after the death of the brave Sten Sture,—had surrendered to King Christian II., but with the stipulation that the King should govern according to the laws of Sweden, and should take no revenge for the obstinate resistance of the Swedes. Christian swore that he would so rule, and partook of the Holy Sacrament in confirmation of his oath. He then visited Sweden, to be crowned in Stockholm. This occurred on the fourth of the present month."

Here the speaker was interrupted by a commotion among the audience, produced by the entrance of a stranger, who forced his way through the crowd to the warm stove, his clothes dripping wet. Rosanna, who stood upon a table, and could overlook the crowd, saw, on glancing around, that her uncle, Bav, had entered simultaneously with the stranger, and had seated himself timidly in a corner.

" The festivities and the banqueting lasted three whole days," continued the narrator, in a loud voice, "and the nobility and the people alike were made to feel secure. But on the morning of the eighth of November, the gates of Stockholm were closed early; all the streets and squares were surrounded by strong Danish guards, and cannon were planted in the market-place. Amidst the clang of trumpets, it was announced that no one should leave his dwelling on pain of death.   Hereupon, the heads of two bishops, of many councilmen, noblemen, and citizens, — ninety-four in all, — fell under the axe of the executioner.   Others were hanged, or put to death in some other cruel manner. The executions continued just as long as the festivities had lasted — until nearly six hundred of the noblest men of Sweden had fallen.   The blood upon the market square flowed in streams into the adjoining streets. Three days long the corpses lay upon the market-place a ghastly spectacle, — priests, nobles, and citizens piled on separate heaps. Thus have fallen the families of Sture, Stoven, Pirker, Vasa — "

At the mention of the latter name, the speaker, as well as the silence of the assembly, was interrupted by a cry of horror and surprise from the stranger beside the stove. He had just before risen from his seat, and had listened to the speaker with intense and constantly increasing interest. This cry was the signal for a general outburst of indignation, and of countless curses and threats against the wicked King.

"Who are you, ill-omened bird?" cried the stranger, as he pressed close to the speaker and seized him by the breast. "Does your mouth really utter the truth?"

"As truly as my name is Lars Olafson, and I am an honest Swede," replied the traveller, firmly. "I have with me a list of the most distinguished of the murdered. There, see for yourself, my countryman!"

The stranger took the paper with a trembling hand, and glanced hastily over the list.

"Oh, my God!" he cried, in his anguish; "my father! my cousins! my brother-in-law! all, all murdered! And I had warned you of Christian's malice and deceit. Why did you not believe me? Oh, that you had turned upon the tyrant at my call!"

"And who are you, my good friend, if I may ask?" said Olafson, with wonder.

"I am Gustavus Erikson, of the house of Vasa," returned the stranger, "upon whose head the King has set a price. Here is that weary head," he continued, to the astonished country people; "who among you thirsts to earn the blood-money? My wretched life is now to me a burden."

"Gustavus Vasa," said Olafson, earnestly, "have a care how you challenge fate. Or, perhaps you think that among the Swedes there is not one who could become your betrayer? Do you murmur at this statement, good Swedes?" continued Olafson. "Well, hear me to the end, and then decide whether I have said too much."

Silently and sadly Gustavus returned to his seat, and Olafson continued:

"After King Christian had ordered the massacre in Stockholm, he repeated the same thing in Finland. His return to Denmark was likewise attended with deeds of cruelty and murder. Thus it was that he redeemed his solemn oath! But I myself was witness, in Jönköping, to a deed without a parallel, by which the tyrant crowned his own infamy. There lived at Jönköping, peacefully, and trusting in the promises of the King, a man with his wife and two sons. This man, Ribbing by name, was pointed out to the tyrant as one who had fought bravely under Sten Sture, and had signed the decree of the Diet against the Archbishop Trolle. Christian at once ordered his execution. His two sons, children of five and eight years of age, were forced to stand close by and witness their father's cruel death. This was fiendish cruelty; but the worst is not yet told. After the murder of the father, Christian, in cold blood, commanded the executioner to behead the two innocent children. The spec-

tators shuddered at hearing the terrible command, and would have prevented its accom-
plishment, had not the great number of
Danish troops rendered resistance impossible. Ah! the two little innocents still remain
before my eyes! Dressed in new blue velvet
jackets, their golden hair hanging in beautiful ringlets, they stood upon the scaffold
beside their dead father. Like a patient
lamb led to the slaughter, the elder boy
knelt at the executioner's command, laid his
head upon the block red with his father's
blood, folded devoutly his dear, delicate little
hands, and quietly awaited the fatal stroke."

Here the speaker was interrupted by the
sobbing of the women and children; but the
men were silent, and looked intently to the
ground.

"When the little Ribbing," continued
Olafson, in a voice trembling with emotion,
"saw himself besprinkled with the blood of

his brother, he awoke from his stupor. He lifted his pale face to the executioner, his eyes swimming in tears, and implored, oh so touchingly, 'Good man, do not stain my clothes thus ; my mother will scold me !'"

Olafson, overcome with emotion, ceased speaking. Even the men now wiped the tears from their eyes, and watched, with ever-increasing interest, the mouth of the speaker, who, after a pause, proceeded :

"The innocent voice touched even the heart of the executioner, and palsied his arm. He let fall the axe, and declared aloud to the King's face, that he would rather die himself than kill the child. Then answered the King, who had sworn to be a father to the people, 'Thy wish shall be granted. Up! first behead the child, and then the refractory executioner!' But, lo! even among the Danes there was not one who would obey the cruel command of the King. Then

Christian, beside himself with anger, looked around, and seeing, in the crowd, a gigantic fellow, with red hair, staring vacantly at him, he cried, 'You fellow! if you would fill your cap with shining dollars, come hither and slay these two. Come, I tell you.' And the man went, and beheaded first the trembling child, and then the compassionate executioner. And he took the blood-money and went away. And this man — hear it, my countrymen! — *this man was a* SWEDE!"

"Let him be accursed!"

These words, which sounded solemnly and threateningly from the lips of every man present, and were re-echoed throughout the apartment, were followed by loud noises in two opposite corners of the room. Here, Rosanna had fallen, with a scream of terror, from the table; there, on the contrary, the table, at which Bav was sitting, burst asunder beneath his thundering blow. The next in-

stant the circle around the speaker was parted
by Bav's powerful arm. If any resisted, they
were hurled to the floor, or pushed aside, till
Bav had forced his way through, and stood
before Olafson. His appearance was fearful
and terrible. His short red hair standing
erect like bristles, his face deathly pale, his
mouth open, and his nostrils distended, his
vest unbuttoned, disclosing his bloody shirt,
his clothing dripping wet — there stood Bav,
with his shirt-sleeves rolled up from his bare
arms. He cast his large, glaring eyes around
the circle, and at last raised his panting voice :

"The King commanded it! And Rosanna
said, 'What the King commands, that we
must do.' Yes, Rosanna said so when
brown Rieke was to be sold. And the
King thought that, because I had the broad-
est back and the largest hands, I could bear
the heavy burden of killing the boy and the
man, with whom I was angry because he had

beheaded the poor little fellow's brother. It
is true the two boys once called me a cannibal; but I have not devoured them; I have
only quietly taken the King's bright dollars
and poured them into Rosanna's apron."

Here Bav ceased, exhausted, and shivering
with cold.

Olafson, who at first supposed that Bav
was insane, did not recognize him at once,
in the dull glimmer of the few torches that
lighted the room. But suddenly he discovered who it was that stood before him.

"This man," cried he, "is the murderer of
the child and of the executioner, and whom
you have just now pronounced *accursed!*"

At these words, a thick circle of strong
arms was extended to seize Bav. The men
prepared for a hard and doubtful struggle,
yet a holy anger overcame their natural
timidity.

But, contrary to the expectation of all,

Bav let himself be taken. He moved not a member of his herculean body to defend himself; on the contrary, he was patient as a sheep. Taking courage from this, the men cried out: "Strike down the monster!. Strangle the Judas Iscariot!"

"Yes, yes!" nodded Bav, a sad smile passing over his face: "strangle me! That would be more kind than if you were to beat me on the head. My head hurts me now without any blows. And since I can no longer eat or drink, why should I live? But even if my old hunger should return, I would have to do, as I did before, steal the hams and sausages from the chimney, and the bread from the oven, and drink the milk and suck the eggs. Then Rosanna would send me back to the copper-mines, where everything tastes so bitter; and then I would have to go to Jönköping to do the King's evil will, and bear such a heavy burden."

7 *

"Make way there!" cried the hindmost in the circle, who appeared with a hastily procured halter wherewith to hang poor Bav. Obedient to the command, the circle opened, when — lo! led by Rosanna's hand, the old pastor stepped among the enraged people.

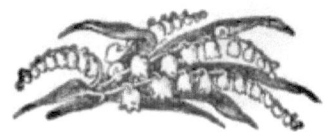

CHAPTER V.

DEFENDING THE CULPRIT.

GOD is not far distant from each and every one of us, but we very often forget His sacred nearness, and disobey His will. And although heaven everywhere arches over us, we yet strive after that which is beneath us, rather than after what is above us. Hence man needs a monitor to remind him of God and of heaven. Such a monitor is, or should be, every faithful minister of the Most High. Such an one was the pastor of Swārdsiō; and, for this reason, the wild clamor was hushed, and the arms lifted to murder fell, as he entered the room. Here he found Bav, and before him stood

Gustavus Vasa, as though he meant to take the imbecile under his protection.

"Peace be with you, my friends!" said the pastor, in solemn tones, saluting the people. "*Blessed are the peacemakers; for they shall be called the children of God. But whosoever is angry with his brother without a cause shall be in danger of the judgment.* What, my friends, are you going to do with this poor creature? Rosanna, here, has told me that you intend to *murder* him? If he has done anything worthy of death, deliver him over to the magistrate and the officer who carries the sword for this purpose."

"But how, reverend sir, if the officer use the sword to kill innocent children — if the King, instead of being a father to his people, is a bloody tyrant?"

"*Fear God, honor the King!*" replied the pastor, admonishingly; "thus saith God's holy Word."

"If the King act in accordance therewith," returned Olafson, warmly. "Decide yourself, whether King Christian deserves to be honored." And he repeated briefly his narrative, at which the pastor was alike astonished and grieved.

"Can it be possible," he cried, "that men — *Christian* men — can act more cruelly than bloodthirsty tigers!" And he raised his eyes with noble wrath to Bav's pale face.

"The King commanded me!" repeated Bav, mournfully; "and I had to bring home much money, so that brown Rieke would not have to be sold. And because my back was so broad and so strong, the King said I could easily bear the little boy and the executioner."

"It is true," replied the pastor, "you should do what the King commands, but only when he commands that which is right. Moreover, we should obey God rather than

F

man. When King Pharaoh commanded the Egyptian midwives to strangle the new-born male children at their birth, they obeyed God rather than the King, in that they permitted the little ones to live; and the Lord rewarded them for this by many blessings. And were there not always wicked men who hasten to obey the unrighteous behests of kings, then would not the children of Bethlehem have been slain by the servants of the cruel Herod, and Rachel would not have wept for her children. Nor would John the Baptist's head have been cut off, and carried on a charger to the false Herodias. And the innocent children of Ribbing would not have fallen by your hand and that of the executioner."

Although Bav could not fully comprehend the pastor's long speech, yet the reproachful tones of his voice, and his own conscience, told him that he had done wrong. He burst into a flood of bitter tears. To see a man weep is ever affecting; and Bav's trembling body, the deep sorrow depicted on his pale face, his bent form, and the mournful tones of his deep voice, spoke touchingly in his favor.

The longer the pastor observed the wretched form before him, the more did his indignation yield to sincere pity. Full of compassion, he again addressed the people.

"My brethren!" he said, sadly, "I deeply deplore, with you, what this unfortunate has done. Yet should we — *dare* we dispute with one who possesses only the outward form of a man, but not the reasoning soul which the Lord Himself breathed into the masterpiece of His creation? Does not Bav resemble a tiger that tears with its powerful claws a tender fawn, though it may be the only treasure, the sole joy of some poor creature? Did not the Apostle Paul once persecute the disciples of Christ? deliver them over to imprisonment and torture? Did he not pursue them with threats and murder, until his ignorance was removed by a voice from heaven? True, we cannot expect from Bav that, like Paul, he will atone for his crime by sacrificing himself, but may he not become, by the grace of God, an instrument by which the good and the right may be exalted? Do you really desire to hurry the poor man, ignorant and unprepared, into the presence of his offended God? Be this far from you!"

"I, too, had intended," said Gustavus Vasa, "to intercede for this man, to whom I owe the preservation of my life. In the darkness, this evening, I had missed the road, and had wandered upon a lake, the ice upon which was not strong enough to bear me. It broke beneath my weight, and I fell into the water up to my neck. I could not see any way of escape. I tried every means, and endeavored by my cries to bring some one to my rescue; and true enough, at the critical moment, this man appeared, who, taking no thought of himself, sprang into the water, took me upon his back, and, swimming with one hand, he shoved the ice before him with the other, and thus we reached the shore. After gaining a firm foothold, he did not permit me to step upon the ground, but carried me to this house, and steadily refused my proffered reward, or even thanks. True, his bloody deed to Ribbing's boy filled me with horror and aversion; yet I felt that I must protect my preserver against the violence of these infuriated men."

"This Bav," said the pastor, thoughtfully, "seems to me like a sharp-edged sword, which, in the hands of a child or a villain, may do much mischief, but, in that of an upright man, can defend innocence and right."

"Ah! reverend sir!" said Gustavus Erik-

son, with a sigh, "your comparison of the
sharp sword recalls to memory my terrible
loss. To lose thus, at one blow, my father
and my dearest relatives! Is there no longer
a just God in heaven, who can avert the
bloody axe from innocent victims and turn it
upon the perjured Christian?"

"It becomes not us, worms of the dust,"
returned the pastor, gently but firmly, "to
wish to understand the unsearchable ways
of the Lord. Only *there* shall we understand that which seems dark to us *here*.
Even in King Christian's case will be ful-
filled the words of the Almighty, ' *Whatso-
ever a man soweth, that shall he also reap.*'
And again, ' *He shall reward every man according to his works !* ' "

And now Rosanna raised her feeble voice.

" Reverend sir!" she said, imploringly,
" see how my poor uncle shivers with cold!
How he staggers, and how his teeth clatter!

His clothes are frozen stiff; surely he will get sick. Do let me take him home. Come, Uncle Bav, and don't be afraid. The pastor has spoken a kind word in your behalf, and this good man also. Won't you please take hold of my uncle, and help move him from the spot; his legs are benumbed?"

The pastor and Gustavus Erikson laid hold of Bav, and took him home to his bed, where, in his present condition, it was fittest for him to be. Gustavus then returned to the inn, where he found a larger crowd than he had left. The spacious room resounded with curses and threats against King Christian and his tyranny. Gustavus improved the favorable opportunity; and, in a speech full of fire and strength, depicted to those present what they might expect in future from Christian's rule; he endeavored to inflame their love of country, and challenged them to unite with him against the tyrant. Nor

did Lars Olafson neglect to fan into a flame
the spark still smouldering under the ashes;
and the two readily prevailed upon their
countrymen to consent with one voice to
join them. But when Gustavus proceeded
to discuss the most judicious way of attack-
ing the Danes, and called upon the peasants
to bring forward the weapons they might
have at hand, and subject them to inspection,
many went away, but did not return. At last
there remained in the inn only a few old men,
who had now to listen to Gustavus Vasa's
vehement denunciation of the faithlessness
and cowardice of the peasantry. They heark-
ened for some time in silence; at last one
of the number rose up and said:

"Herre Erikson! you are a young, hot-
headed man, without wife, children, or other
near relatives. You have nothing more to
risk but a few inches of your neck, which
you can easily draw, at the right time, out of

the noose. With us it is quite a different thing. In a contest with King Christian we might lose everything — house, farm, cattle, wives, and children, and our heads besides. Christian has not yet done *us* any harm. Why then should we trouble ourselves about the wrongs of others? Now you have our opinion, which the rest did not wish to express openly before you. The peasants are the lowest in rank, why should they be the first to take the field? Turn to your equals, Herre Erikson!"

At this plain declaration, Gustavus left the house in a passion, and would have travelled further the same night, had not his wet clothing, his fatigue, and a fearful snow-storm prevented. So he found himself once more in the house of the widow Mindson, and at the side of Bav's bed, which was now a sick-bed, for Bav, poor Bav, lay there all unconscious.

8 *

CHAPTER VI.

GREAT DANGERS.

BAV had been attacked by a raging fever, which caused his mind to wander; and, in his delirium, the scene of the execution of the little Ribbings was almost the only thing of which he spoke.

"How often," said Fru Mindson to the pastor, who had come to visit the sick man, "has my brother-in-law brought the wild ducks out of the ice-cold water in winter time, and worn his wet clothing without the slightest injury to his health. And yet, while Herre Erikson, who certainly is no hardier than Bav, remains so hearty, poor Bav must be seized with such severe sickness."

"This is very natural, Fru, as I will explain to you," replied the pastor. "It is not the body, but the soul of your brother-in-law that is sick. Not alone on Mount Sinai and upon two tables of stone has the Lord God made known his commands — no! He has also written them in letters of fire on every human heart. There the most ignorant, even the silly Bav, can — nay, *must* — read them. And not only read, but obey them. If we neglect this, and make unto ourselves a golden image for a God, then the law knocks at the heart of the sinner, as though written on tables of stone. This is the malady of your brother-in-law, which the physical exposure only helped to develop more speedily. Hence his timorous look, his want of appetite, his burning thirst, his restlessness, his loss of sleep."

"Then must King Christian have no peaceful moments," said Rosanna, naively.

"All human hearts are not alike," returned
the pastor; "that of your uncle, as you can
see, is still tender. But many a heart is surrounded by a hard, solid crust, against which
the law has often to strive for years before it
breaks. Yes, many a man possesses, to his
misfortune, a heart so hardened that even the
iron hand of death cannot break the crust
about it. Such a heart as this the irresisti-
ble flames of hell alone can melt. How it
may be with King Christian's heart, we indeed cannot know; but this much we *do*
know, that God permits neither Himself nor
His holy word to be mocked."

The good pastor then left, promising to
return again soon; and Rosanna and her
brother Henrik accompanied him to the
door, while Fru Mindson remained by the
sick man. Gustavus Vasa, who, owing to
the inclement weather, and for the sake of
security, still tarried in the friendly house of

Fru Mindson, now entered the room, in the dress of a servant, and relieved Fru Mindson at Bav's bedside.

Suddenly Henrik rushed in.

"The Danes!" he cried, almost breathless. "The Danes are riding into the village! They occupy all the roads, and are going into the farm-houses in bands. They will come here, too!"

At these words, Gustavus Vasa looked composedly at his hostess, and as if inquiring what should be done.

As she showed no signs of fear, Gustavus asked deliberately, "Do you think, Fru, there can be any one in the village who could wish to earn the price set upon my head?"

"I do not fear it," said Fru Mindson, "because, if they should betray your presence, they are all liable to be brought to account for the vehement curses and threats they uttered against King Christian on the evening of your arrival. Henrik, leave the room, and go with Rosanna to the pastor's. I need not caution you to keep silence. And you, Herre, when you hear the Danes approach, run to the fireplace. The rest will be plain enough."

They did not have long to wait for the Danes. Three men rushed, noisy and blustering, into the room, which they searched thoroughly.

"Well, what are you looking for?" cried Fru Mindson, sharply, as she rose from her seat beside the sick-bed. "Can you not step more softly: I have a sick man lying here? It's well for you, too, that he *is* sick. If he were well, he'd soon make you take to your heels. What dirt you impudent fellows have dragged into the room. What *is* the use of one's cleaning up?"

"Silence, you spit-fire," cried one of the Danes, angrily, while the other two laughed.

"Who is this sick man? Is he not disguising himself? What's that he's muttering about cutting off heads, and a blue velvet jacket?"

"I must be silent, must I?" angrily retorted Fru Mindson. "'Who is he?' Do you know him no longer? He is King Christian's best executioner, and my brother-in-law. It was he who beheaded little Ribbing and the refractory executioner at Jönköping. Were you not there? He dreams of it in his delirium even now, as you hear."

"Markoff," said one of the soldiers, "the woman speaks the truth. "I recognize the fellow by his red hair and his broad shoulders. Ha! Gustavus Vasa would never flee to this man's house!"

"Who knows!" returned Markoff, looking sharply at Erikson, who stood near the fire. "I see another man yonder, who is not unlike the description."

"By my faith!" cried Fru Mindson, turn-

ing round with well-feigned astonishment,
" there stands that idle drone again, warming
his lazy fingers at the fire."

As she spoke, she darted towards Erikson,
seized a piece of wood lying in her way, and
struck the pretended servant heavy blows
across the shoulders, scolding as she did so.

" You lazy clown, have you nothing better
to do than to stand here making big eyes?
Is there no work for you? Can you not, at
least, carry in an armful of wood? Must I
always be worrying and vexing myself about
such things, when I have my sick brother-in-
law to attend to?"

Erikson, grumbling, skulked sneakingly
out of the room.

" This is not our man!" said the second
soldier. " If this were Gustavus Vasa, he
would not have suffered himself to be beaten
over the shoulders by a peasant witch, even
at the sacrifice of freedom and of life."

"Come, comrades! let us look elsewhere," cried the third, "lest some one else should catch the bird."

They started to go, and before the door they met Gustavus laden with a bundle of brushwood. Markoff gave him a push from behind, so that Gustavus and his load plunged headlong into the room.

The push accomplished that which Fru Mindson's heavy blows could not. Gustavus's noble blood boiled; regardless of consequences, his first impulse was for vengeance. But, as he was hastening out of the room to avenge himself on his assailant, he was held back by the strong hand of his hostess.

"Guard your life for your Fatherland," she said to him, firmly. "Stake it not against that of a miserable Danish blackguard. Of myself and family, whom you would endanger equally with yourself, I will say nothing."

9   G

No more was needed to cool Erikson's ill-timed anger. He thanked his hostess heartily for her counsel, and promised that he would some day prove, by his deeds, his gratitude for her interest in his welfare.

In a few days the sick Bav grew better. He again had lucid moments, and enjoyed refreshing slumbers. On the contrary, Erikson's safety was becoming more and more imperilled by his sojourn at the widow Mindson's. The report was current that Gustavus Vasa was wandering about in the neighborhood, was rousing the people to resistance to Danish oppression, and endeavoring to persuade them to revolt. Gustavus determined, therefore, to leave the house of his hostess, so that she would not be endangered, and to flee deeper into the mountain fastnesses. But the execution of this latter determination was prevented by the pastor, who offered to take the fugitive into his house, which was less exposed to the danger of being searched by the Danes than was Fru Mindson's. Here Gustavus Vasa remained for eight days, but with ever increasing danger, which at last determined the good pastor to detain the pursued fugitive in Swärdsiö no longer.

Early one December morning, before the dawn of day, Fru Mindson's yard-gate opened, and a farmer's wagon, well laden with straw, and drawn by two horses, passed out. Bav, who was now well again, drove; beside him, in the straw, sat Rosanna. Despite the early hour, many people were afoot, who, astonished at seeing Bav, cried out, " Good luck, Bav! are you quite well again? You look thin. Whither are you going so early in the morning ? ".

" To market, at Rättwick," answered Rosanna for Bav, " where the straw will sell for more than with us. My mother needs money."

"What!" exclaimed one, "are the sixty dollars already gone which Bav got for —?"

"Oh, do not mention it!" begged Rosanna, "if you would not make my uncle sick again. It was not kind in you, Kunas, to say that."

Kunas went on his way, muttering, and Rosanna and Bav turned the horses upon the road that led to Rättwick. As the sun rose in the cloudless sky, the snow glistened like sparkling dew-drops in summer.

"If there were only more snow," said Rosanna, "we could take the sled and travel much faster. Dear Bav, how are you? Do you feel cold? Do you feel any return of your sickness? Oh, do speak!"

Bav looked at Rosanna, tried to smile, and shook his head in silence. Then he swung his whip, and urged on his horses, until they were soon covered with foam.

"You crack the whip too often, Bav," said

Rosanna. "You will drive the horses too hard, and ruin them."

"You are right," said Bav; "but, as long as I swing the whip, he goes away; but he soon comes back."

"Who?" inquired Rosanna, somewhat surprised.

Bav was silent. After a short struggle with himself, he said, in low tones: "The little Ribbing with the golden locks."

"No, no!" said Rosanna, stoutly. "This is all imagination, and proceeds from your sickness."

Again Bav shook his head.

"The pastor has assured you," said Rosanna, "that, inasmuch as you have done the deed through ignorance, God will forgive you; and He certainly will if you repent, and show, by your future good deeds, your sorrow for the past. You have made a good beginning by saving the life of Erikson."

9 *

"If I only knew what was good and what bad," sighed Bav. "*You* know, Rosanna; stay with me always, and I will do as you tell me."

"Herre Erikson knows better than I," replied Rosanna, modestly. "Do whatever *he* bids you. But hark, Bav! do you not hear the tramping of horses? Look! yonder come the Danish troopers."

Bav looked well pleased. He put his right hand under his fur coat, and asked:

"Shall I draw, Rosanna, and kill them? Ha! the little Ribbing is gone now!"

"Don't get excited, Bav!" implored Rosanna. "Let me speak. Do you do no more at most than to repeat my words. Do you hear?"

In a moment the Danes were beside the wagon.

"Whence have you come? Whither are you going?" they demanded, peremptorily.

"From Swärdsiö — to Rättwick — to the market," answered Rosanna.

"To market," growled Bav, in the deepest bass.

"Have you nothing in your wagon but straw?"

"No!" said Rosanna. "What else should we have?"

"Have!" echoed Bav.

"Have you seen anything of a fellow by the name of Gustavus Erikson?" asked the men, further. "He has brown hair, a long and somewhat crooked nose, and goes about disguised as a farmer's man. He must be somewhere in this neighborhood."

"I saw a man, dressed as a farmer's man, about a quarter of an hour since, running towards the forest of Skensiö," said Rosanna; "but whether his name is Gustavus Erikson or not, I cannot say."

"Say!" repeated Bav.

"I wish you could put us on the right
track!" said one of the troopers. " The
King has set a high price on Erikson's head,
and a portion of it would then be yours!"

Here Bav looked suddenly sad, and said,
gloomily, to Rosanna: "There he is again
already!"

" Who?" inquired the horseman.

"Ah!" said Rosanna, "it is a sad story.
My uncle, here, by command of King Christian, had to kill the little Ribbing, and ever
since he constantly sees the little fellow before
him."

" Before him!" groaned Bav.

The men looked at each other doubtfully.

"Well," said one, "let us, at least, search
through the straw. Help me throw off the
top layer?"

The troopers drew their sabres, and with
them tossed the bundles of straw from the
wagon. Through the layers that remained

they thrust their sharp weapons up to the hilt, at which Rosanna grew pale and red by turns; but, fortunately, the soldiers did not notice her.

"Well," said one of the troopers, "if he's sticking in there, he must have very little feeling, for he'd be as full of holes as a sieve. Let us be off."

With this they galloped away.

Bav and Rosanna had alighted from the wagon, and were busy replacing the straw which the Danes had thrown off, but had not taken the trouble to put on again. As the latter was picking up a bundle, she asked, in suppressed tones: "In God's name, Herre Erikson! are you alive or dead?"

"Alive!" was the hollow reply from beneath the straw; "but wounded in the leg. Move on, however, and do not be uneasy about me."

As soon as the straw was replaced upon

the wagon, they proceeded. Rosanna was
walking behind. Suddenly she exclaimed:
"Alas! here's blood, Herre Erikson: you
are bleeding so much that the blood is drop-
ping through the wagon."

"Never mind — never mind," said Gustavus.

"But the blood," replied the thoughtful
girl, "will betray you!"

"True," returned Gustavus; "but we cannot think of bandaging the wound now. For
who knows but that the patrol is watching
us from a distance, or that another is coming
upon us? Let Bav stick one of the horses
in the thigh," he continued, after a little reflection, "so that it may look as if the blood
had flowed from it."

"In the thigh?" said Rosanna. "Oh, no!
the horse would then become lame, and we
could move on but slowly. Bav, cut off the
tail of one of the horses! Uncle has been

guilty of so many silly tricks, that nobody will be particularly astonished at this one."

Bav, in obedience to Rosanna's command, took his large knife, and, seizing the horse's tail in his left hand, cut it off with his right; but he kept his eyes closed while doing so; and for the remainder of the journey he turned his eyes away from the horses, for he could not endure the sight of blood.

They arrived, without further molestation, at the town of Rättwick, which lies scattered between high mountains. The pastor had commended the fugitive to his colleague in this place; and, therefore, the wagon was driven to the parsonage, which was near the church, and was some distance from the other houses. Gustavus Vasa had lost much blood; the straw was saturated with it, where it had soaked through upon the ground as they drove along. When the deep flesh wound had been dressed with considerable skill by the pastor, Rosanna said to the wounded man :

"How the thrust must have pained you, Herre Erikson! Had it happened to me, I would have screamed out; but you did not stir."

"A man," replied Gustavus Vasa, with a smile, "must know how to master pain. Loud screams from pain are excusable in children and in women, but not in a strong man, and especially a soldier."

"Mind that, Bav!" said Rosanna. "For if any one happens to give you a thump on your great, tall body, you stretch open your mouth like a barn-door."

"But when I get one on my head," replied Bav, " I *must* scream."

"You *must?*" returned Gustavus Vasa. "Who, then, compels you? Man is free, and, if he wills it, he need not cry out even in the anguish of death."

"Yes, that is true," said Bav, with a sigh; "even the little Ribbings did not cry out when they were executed."

"I will now drive home," said Rosanna, "before nightfall. Farewell, Herre Erikson; be kind, I beg of you, to my uncle. And you, Bav, obey Herre Erikson in everything. Give me your hand, Bav! Mind—in everything."

"Oh, stay with me," implored Bav. "Henrik will be home to help your mother."

"No," said Gustavus Vasa; "the road through the rough mountain before us is not for a child to travel. There will be difficulties and dangers to surmount that might well appall a man. Think of this now, Bav, and turn back while you may."

Bav looked at Rosanna inquiringly.

"Have you already forgotten, Bav, what you should do? That you should make good the evil you have done? Go, Bav, and

don't hesitate or falter. God be with you,
my poor uncle."

Bav manfully obeyed, and remained stead-
fastly with Gustavus Erikson, who used every
effort, but in vain, as he had done in Swärdsiö, to incite the Dalecarlians to revolt against
Christian.   His eloquence was wasted on the
timid countrymen, who, because they themselves had suffered but little by Christian's
tyranny, thought they had not a sufficient
pretext for revolt. Every effort to arouse the
people against his oppressor endangered his
personal safety still more, and he was compelled at last to resume his flight. Before
his wound was thoroughly healed, he left
Rättwick, accompanied by Bav, intending to
try his fortune with the rougher Norwegians
across the mountains. This was in the
depth of winter — a Norwegian winter.

CHAPTER VII.

THE BETRAYER.

THE wind was rough and cold. It brought with it a shower of fine snow, which pricked the uncovered skin like needle-points. The sun had long since sunk, red as blood, beneath the horizon, and naught save the whiteness of the snow relieved the dark twilight. Two men were wandering upon a succession of hills which enclosed a narrow valley like the sides of a bowl. The breath from their mouths had congealed upon their beards and moustaches like white frost; and their high boots, reaching to their knees, were covered with a hard crust of snow.

"There, Herre!" said one of the men, in whom we at once recognize the giant Bav;

"yonder is what we have been looking for so long!"

What can be more cheering to the wanderer, who has long lost his way, is hungry, cold, and weary, than the sight of a friendly light shining towards him through the darkness? How secure, how sheltered from the storm, seemed the country-seat, with its farm-houses well protected by a high wall against the wild animals which lurked in the gorge! How quickly could the weary limbs now descend the mountain sides! how vigorously the benumbed hands could knock upon the gate! The barking of dogs answered the appeal for admission. Soon the snow creaked beneath the heavy tread of a man; a small window opened in the wall, and a rough-looking face peered out, asking in a gruff tone, "What do you want? Who are you?"

"Since when," replied Gustavus Vasa, re-

proachfully, " has it become the mode in Sweden, and especially in the hospitable mountains, that the name and purpose of belated
travellers is asked before admitting them?
Is not your master a Swede or a Christian?"

At this question the man grumbled somewhat, but he opened the gate and admitted
the wayfarers. He stared at the gigantic Bav
with open-mouthed astonishment. As Gustavus and Bav were dressed in but ordinary
clothing, they were led into the buildings
occupied by the farm-hands, in which they
found a well-warmed room, and were straightway supplied with a good meal.

Bav soon showed that he had not entirely
lost his former appetite. He devoured so
much food that those present looked at him
with laughter and amazement, and even the
owner of the property became curious to see
him. He was a nobleman, and was well ac-
quainted with Gustavus Vasa, whom he at

once recognized, and introduced to his family as his *friend*.

"You see, dear Erikson," said he, "I live here with my wife, my children, and my servants, entirely shut out from the world, and hence learn little or nothing of what is going on. Tell me, my friend, how you are getting along, and how matters stand at present with our Fatherland? First of all, why do you wear these servants' clothes? and why wander afoot in winter through this desolate country?"

"I know not, dear Persson," answered Erikson, "whether I should congratulate or pity you upon your ignorance. 'How is it with our Fatherland?' Bad—bad, do I say! hopeless! Our unhappy country bleeds beneath the oppression of a perjured tyrant, the cruel Christian! Know you not of the massacre of Stockholm, which cost the lives of six hundred of Sweden's noblest sons, and among them my father, my brother-in-law, and my cousins? Know you not that Denmark's king, in his thirst for blood, spares not even innocent children? See how your dear children play around their mother, and hang upon her looks and lips. Two children, innocent as these, the King ordered to be executed at Jönköping, and the executioner, too, because he possessed a heart more human than that of the tyrant."

"Terrible! horrible!" exclaimed the wife of the nobleman, as she pressed her children closer to her.

"But," said Persson, "how is it that you are in Sweden? Had you not been taken as a hostage to Denmark?"

"Yes," returned Gustavus Vasa; "and I was held a prisoner in violation of all international law. I lived there under the protection of a relative who had freed me from prison by becoming my surety. But when I

heard of the treachery of Christian, who
wished to take possession of my country by
force of arms, I escaped, and fled, first to
Lübeck, whose council protected me from
my pursuers, and promised me assistance in
money and men in case I should succeed in
arousing my countrymen to resistance against
the Danes.   But, with the death of the brave
Sten Sture, Sweden's confidence and courage
fell.   Go where I might, my efforts were fruitless.   In Calmar, the German garrison threatened to deliver me up to the Danes ; and to
turn my steps towards Stockholm, I dared
not venture. Surrounded by dangers on
every hand, I wandered through Smaland
and Südermanland, passing the nights in the
grain-fields or in the woods. Even my brother-in-law wished not to hear of me ; and my
sister begged me, with tears, to desist from
my dangerous purpose. Wherever I made
myself known, the doors were closed against

me; and even the cloister of Gripsholm, founded by my ancestors, refused me an asylum. I resolved at last to go to the Dalecarlians, in the mountains, among whom I hoped still to find simple customs, love of country, and freedom, bravery, hospitality, and rectitude. Nor was I altogether mistaken. I was hospitably received; my speeches were applauded; and I was concealed from my pursuers: but even the Dalecarlians would not follow me to battle against the Danes. I have thus become like a hunted wild beast, which, to escape from the pursuing Danes, endeavors to escape into Norway. This, good Persson, is my story."

"How I sympathize with you!" exclaimed Persson, with feeling. "Would that I could assist you! But you must tarry with me; and not leave my house, at least, till I have learned whether you can continue your jour-

ney to Norway without danger. In which
direction do you purpose going ?"

"Across Slemwick and Törnebock," answered Gustavus Vasa; "for I must avoid
every place that is garrisoned by Danish
soldiers."

"But," cried Persson, "let us dismiss all
care to-day, and let us trust and pray for the
deliverance of our dear Fatherland."

The two friends sat together till late, and
Gustavus retired to his couch with a head
somewhat heavy. The comfortable bed,
together with his excessive fatigue, caused
him to sleep soundly. He would have slept
till broad daylight, had he not been awakened
early in the morning by Bav's heavy hand.
He had passed the night in a different apartment, but yet could go unhindered into the
room in which Gustavus slept; for, at that
time, and especially in this region, only
wooden latches were used in the houses.

"Herre," said Bav, "it is day. Are we not to go farther, as we intended yesterday?"

Before Gustavus could answer his companion, there was heard a slight noise in the yard beneath. Bav walked to the window, and grumbled, "Look, Herre! our host is up and stirring earlier than we."

Gustavus leaped from his bed, and saw that Persson was about to leave the yard, accompanied by two servants. All three moved around with the greatest caution.

"Whither so early, friend Persson?" cried Gustavus, from the window.

"Oho!" returned Persson, with a laugh. "I thought you were still fast asleep. Why do you not rest longer? In order that you may remain more than this one night under my roof, I mean to search the neighborhood, and see whether any one suspects your presence. In a few hours I shall return. Till then, act as if you were in your own house.

I have directed my wife to provide for your every wish. Good morning, friend Erikson."

Once awake, Gustavus could not again close his eyes. As he saw a bright light in the family sitting-room, he crossed over to it, when Bav had returned to the servants' apartment, and found his hostess busily preparing breakfast.

" It is for my sake," he said, after saluting her, " that Persson has left you so early. I am sorry for this; yet I know that I am always a burden to my hosts."

" You know, then ? " stammered the confused woman.

" Yes : he admitted this, when I expressed my astonishment at his early departure."

" And what will you do now ? " asked Fru Persson, trembling.

" Under the protection of your hospitality, I shall patiently wait for the news your husband may bring. He thought," added

Gustavus, "that he would return in a few hours."

"Yes, this was his intention," said Fru Persson. "The place nearest to us is Neerholm, where there lives a sister of my husband, the wife of a Danish officer. Owing to the present bad condition of the roads, one can scarcely go thither and return in four hours."

"Your husband, of course, is in a position to learn the latest news concerning my pursuers and my safety. But are your dear children still asleep."

"They are still sleeping soundly and sweetly," returned Fru Persson, sorrowfully. "Look at them," she added, as she drew aside a curtain, behind which the two children were sound asleep upon their bed.

"May God Almighty take you under his protection," said Gustavus, making the sign of the cross over the young sleepers; "and may you fare better than I have. Yes, my dear woman! it was never sung beside my cradle that I should one day lose my father and my relatives by the axe of the executioner, and that I myself should become a hunted outlaw, who should fall at last into the hands of his pursuers. In that case I would fare worse than did my father; for, not without a weighty reason, has King Christian set so large a price upon my head."

Fru Persson sighed, and tears stood in her eyes.

"Will you not partake of your breakfast?" she asked.

Gustavus approached the table, saying:

"How rejoiced I am, after so many sad experiences, to find, in your husband, a friend whom no narrow-minded views can influence, and one who will work for me faithfully and disinterestedly."

To this Fru Persson made no reply; she

stepped to the window, then to the bed of her children; a great struggle was going on in her mind, which, from the changing expression of her countenance, would not have escaped the notice of a more watchful observer than the trustful Gustavus, who continued to eat and drink, suspecting nothing. Suddenly the hostess laid both her hands upon his shoulders, and cried, in a voice half choked with tears:

"Gustavus Erikson! flee — *as you value your life, leave this house!* Here, you will be taken prisoner!"

"How? Do I hear aright?" exclaimed Gustavus, in surprise. "Ha! is your husband a dastardly traitor?"

"He is a weak man," said Fru Persson, "and somewhat greedy of gain. He dreads King Christian's revenge. Add to this his near relationship to the Danish officer, and the high price set upon your head."

"But," asked Gustavus, "why did not your husband surprise me in **my** sleep, and bind me hand and foot? Why does he call upon strangers to assist him, when there are servants enough here of his own to overpower me? I ask, therefore, are you quite sure that you are not mistaken?"

"I am only too certain!" said Fru Persson. "In a matter like this he dared not trust his servants, who are all honorable Swedes; and, besides, he feared the resistance of your gigantic companion. He wished, also, to avoid the appearance of having taken you prisoner with his own hands, and of violating the sacred rights of hospitality."

"The villain and traitor ever acts thus," said Gustavus, fiercely. "He seeks to avoid only the appearance of evil — not evil itself."

"Spare your reproaches," implored the wife; "but flee! my husband may be even now at Neerholm."

"How can I flee," asked Erikson, bitterly, "through the deep snow, and with my wounded leg?"

"Take from our stable," said Fru Persson, "a swift horse and a sleigh. My husband will think that you became suspicious, and determined upon a speedy flight, which I, a weak woman, could not prevent. Should any of the servants venture to interfere with you, remind them of what my husband said to you. Make haste; I beg of you, make haste!"

Gustavus ran to the servants' room, and inquired of one of them which was the fastest horse in the stable.

"Well, really," replied the man, "our master took the fastest horse this morning; yet there's the brown stallion, the roan, and even 'the fox,' with the white spot, which takes by far the longest steps, and does not soon tire."

"Good!" said Gustavus; "hitch either one

of the three to a sleigh, and you shall have this bright dollar."

"I'll do it without that," returned the servant, good-naturedly. He started off, but soon returned shaking his head resentfully.

"The surly Kätthist," he informed the impatient Gustavus, "asserts that the brown stallion has the spavin, that the roan is foundered, and that 'the fox,' too, has something the matter with him. All this must have happened during the night, for last evening they were all perfectly sound."

Greatly enraged, Gustavus hastened to the stable; within the door, in a lazy attitude, stood the morose watcher of the night before. "What do you want?" he asked, in an insulting tone.

"That you must find out from your mistress, fellow," answered Gustavus, as he pushed aside the servant, despite his immense size.

" Bav! Bav!" he called.

Bav came, and Gustavus ordered him to select the lightest sleigh, and draw it out of the shed into the yard. He examined, meantime, the condition of the stallion, on which he could find no sign of spavin. In a few moments the horse was harnessed to the sleigh, which Bav and Erikson then entered.

All the domestics surrounded the two who were about to leave, and who were already seated in the sleigh.

"There, my good fellow," said Gustavus, throwing the promised dollar to the servant; "now open the gate for us."

"As you value your life," said Kätthist, angrily, "do not undertake it." At the same instant he seized the impatient horse by the reins. "Our master," he continued, "expressly commanded that, until he returned, no one, be he who he might, should leave the yard; much less with any of his property."

"Let go, villain!" said Gustavus, coolly; "or you will bitterly repent it."

"Oho!" sneered Kätthist; "you count, perhaps, on the big fellow beside you. Well, he has shown himself to be brave and strong by his valiant attacks upon full dishes and great loaves. But I'll make short work of this. Know, comrades, this man, who will do so much, is an outlaw, a criminal, and a rebel, for whose capture King Christian has offered a large reward. Lucky are we that we have entrapped so rare a mouse. Let us seize the fellow, and fill our pockets with pure, bright dollars! Lay to, men, I tell you!"

As the servants stood irresolute, and no one seemed willing to be the first to move, Kätthist let go the horse's reins to begin the attack.

"Bav!" said Gustavus, showing no signs of fear, "it is now time to silence the babbler.

But, if possible, spare the poor creature's life."

Bav got quietly out of the sleigh, seized Kätthist by the breast as he approached, threw him up so as to catch him by the foot, swung the big fellow around a few times in the air, and then hurled him from him with such force that he lay on the ground insensible. Having performed this Herculean feat in silence, Bav drew from under his coat a large knife, and held it towards the crowd.

"We are faithful Dalecarlians, and no traitors," said the oldest among them. Whereupon Bav, at a sign from Gustavus, sheathed his knife and entered the sleigh. The servant, meantime, to whom Gustavus had given the dollar, had opened the gate. Gustavus greeted the nobleman's wife, who was looking out of the window, and cried to her:

"Accept my hearty thanks, my noble lady,

for your hospitality; and be assured, I shall never forget what you — what your husband has done for me.   Farewell!"

The whip cracked, and the good horse sped away with his precious load.

CHAPTER VIII.

DIVERS ENEMIES.

PERSSON was, indeed, such a miserable betrayer, that he had hastened to his brother-in-law, at Neerholm, and had told him of Erikson's presence in his house. The Danish officer started at once with twenty men, and rode, with all possible haste, to Persson's country-seat, where, however, he discovered with chagrin that the bird had flown. He immediately ordered his men to pursue the fugitives. Meantime, Gustavus Vasa had taken quite a different road towards Norway from that which he had told the treacherous Persson he would take. As soon as the horse became too much fagged to travel fast, Gustavus left him in charge of a

farmer, with the request that both horse and
sleigh should be returned to the owner; but
not for three days. This the honest Dalecarlian promised to do, and he kept his word.
As the path, which the two fugitives had now
to travel, led through rocky chasms, over
steep precipices, and through thick forests,
they were forced to continue their journey
entirely on foot.

They had travelled thus till evening, when
they found themselves in a desolate wilder-
ness, where they might well hope to be safe
from human pursuit, but where, on the other
hand, they had all the more to fear from wild
beasts, among which were ravenous wolves.
Their evening song — a fearful howling —
could already be heard in the distance. The
travellers soon perceived numerous fiery orbs
shining out of the dark thicket: could
they be aught but the eyes of wolves? And
now one of these dangerous animals planted

himself in the middle of the path, and could only be driven away by the loud cries of the fugitives.

Then it was that Gustavus Vasa exclaimed: "I would rather dwell among wolves and bears than fall into the hands of King Christian and his hangmen. For that wicked man is more bloodthirsty and cruel than the most rapacious beast."

"You are right," said Bav; "for would the wicked King Christian have gone so quickly out of your way as the wolf did?"

"If he had been alone," returned Erikson, with a smile, "he would have left much faster. For a tyrant ever hides behind his hired servants."

"Herre!" said Bav, looking cautiously around, "it may be that the chased wolf may call together his uncles and cousins, and come back with them. It's a pity that I must dull my knife on the throats of these

beasts instead of the Danes! What think
you, Herre?"

The reader will perceive that Bav now
speaks more connectedly and more sensibly
than in the beginning of our narrative. In
the school of danger, under the stern tuition
of necessity and experience, one learns far
more rapidly than in ordinary every-day life;
and Bav's former life had been chiefly spent
among cows and oxen.

"We will kindle a fire, and drive away the
wolves," said Gustavus Vasa. "We can also
light our torches, that we may the better pursue our way. Look, Bav! in the underbrush,
yonder, glow no less than four pairs of fiery
eyes!"

Bav, who carried under his arm several
pine-knots, halted, took out his tin box, in
which were steel, flint, and tinder, and,
striking fire, ignited two of them. Gustavus
took one, and Bav, holding the other before

him, walked up to the thicket in which the pack of wolves were lurking. The tender, dried branches of young wood that were above the snow speedily ignited, and the flames spread rapidly; but, as there was no abundance of inflammable matter, the fire soon spent itself. However, the affrighted wolves had run away, and did not again venture to molest the belated wanderers.

On they travelled, granting themselves but little rest. The obstacles in their way—the deep snow, the high mountains, the pathless forest, the darkness, and the rough winter weather — were great, but could not deter our hardy Swedes. The picture of our two travellers, and their surroundings, would be well worth delineating. The giant Bav, torch in hand, led the way. Lighted up by the lurid, flickering rays, the rocky walls projected sharp and rugged, while the dark ravines seemed all the darker. Thick woods,

whose tall trees bowed their branches beneath the heavy burden of snow, stood there
threatening and silent; occasionally the crash
of a bough, breaking beneath its weight of
snow, smote sharply upon the ear, but the
noise died away in a hollow murmur. Where
the uneven ground could be seen, it resembled a graveyard in winter-time; the low,
solitary bushes resembling black, monu-
mental crosses. Over the landscape hung
the dark-blue winter sky, studded with countless stars, which, however, were dimmed by
the silvery light of the full moon.

"Are you tired, Bav, or hungry?" asked
Gustavus Vasa, at midnight, of his companion, who had walked a long time in
silence.

"No, Herre!" was the answer.

"Why, then, are you so quiet?" returned
Gustavus.

Bav sighed deeply, and said: "Well, Herre,

when I am going along leisurely, then — then my wicked deed recurs to my mind. Would you believe me, the very moon above us looks to me as if it were the little Ribbing! It has the same curly locks, the same sad face. If only I could have an opportunity to strike the Danes!"

"That may soon happen," returned Gustavus. "But would to God that the cruel Christian felt the same stings of conscience that you feel! You bear them instead of him. When will you become comforted? We all have justified your act; and even the pastor has assured you of forgiveness."

"I know," replied Bav; "and yet the little Ribbing will not leave me."

Here the conversation ended, and each continued the journey in silence. As they no longer heard the howling of the wolves, and the moon had risen higher and now shone quite brightly, the wanderers had ex-

12 *

tinguished their torches. At last, tired nature asserted her rights; Gustavus Vasa felt the need of rest. So, as he descried a dark hole in a rock, which seemed to be the entrance to a cave, he said, " Bav, let us tarry here, and gather fresh strength. This cave seems well suited for our purpose, and, if it be large enough to lie down in, we will take possession."

As Bav stooped to enter the cave, he stumbled over something lying in the entrance, which rolled aside with a hollow sound.

"A stag's head!" growled Bav, as he investigated the cause of his stumbling. "Aye, Herre! what say you to that?"

" Nothing !" replied Gustavus: " what should I say about it?"

"Well, I think," said Bav; " nay, I should say I *know*. — I have sometimes gone hunting for bears."

" And what of that?"

" Only this; that when we found stag bones, or any other bones, the hunters said that the bears were not far distant."

" You are right, Bav! I understand you now," said Gustavus. "Let us be careful, and explore the cave before we lie down in it."

Bav lighted his torch again and crept into the cave, at the same time cautioning Gustavus to remain outside till he had completed the search. This Gustavus did, and Bav, having looked into the cave, reported:

" There are a great many bones in the cave, and an elegant bed of leaves, but no bear — he has gone on a hunt. How astonished he will be when he returns and finds his den occupied; ha, ha!"

The cave was dry, and sheltered from the rough wind. It was agreed upon that one should remain awake, and watch at the mouth of the cave for the return of the "proprietor," while the other slept. Much as Bav slept

formerly, and much as he wished to sleep
now, yet he refused to be the first to lie down
upon the leafy couch; and Erikson occupied
the soft bed. Bav, on the other hand, gathered together some dry wood, and kindled a
fire at the entrance of the cave, which kept
them comfortably warm.

Bav sat beside the fire, his broad back
turned towards the sleeper in the corner, and
stared into the crackling flames. Suddenly
he seized a brand and hurled it in the air.

"I am satisfied at last," he growled.
"Herre Erikson sleeps soundly," he continued, in a low tone; "he snores like an ass.
Heugh! he must be dreaming, he seems so
restless. And he can growl, too, equal to a
bear! and now he chokes, as if he were swallowing sea-water. Ha!" he exclaimed, and,
turning towards the sleeper, he descried a
large, dark object standing over him, which
he recognized at once to be a — bear!

How he got into the cave, Bav did not stop to inquire. To seize the long hunter's knife lying beside him, and rush with it upon the unwelcome visitor, was the work of an instant. As soon as the animal felt the point of the knife in his side, he turned upon his assailant with a terrible growl, quitting at the same time his position on Erikson's body. Gustavus felt as if a mountain had been taken off his breast, the weight of which had almost suffocated him. Raising himself up, but yet half unconscious, he perceived a singular rider, in a stooping posture, rushing past the fire and out of the cave.

Some minutes elapsed before Gustavus had entirely recovered his senses and could go to the entrance of the cave. Bav came running to him, smiling.

"Are you wounded, Bav?" asked Gustavus.

"If you are not, then I am not."

"But how did it happen? Speak, Bav!"

"I don't know," said Bav, "whether the
brown rascal had been sleeping under the
leaves, or whether he knew of some other
entrance. I thought, all the time, that it was
you that was snoring and growling so loudly,
till I heard you choking. There lay, or sat,
or stood, the bear upon your body, just as if
he had a right to be there! And when I
struck him between the ribs with my knife,
he ran upon me so madly that I could do
nothing but spring upon his back and clutch
him by the neck. Before I had time to turn
around and get a firm seat in my saddle, we
were both out of the cave like a shot. I
was, no doubt, the first rider my horse ever
had on his back, for he ran as if possessed,
and would have carried me over the precipice,
had I not plunged my knife into his neck in
the nick of time. Yes, Herre, in Swärdsiö
I had often to be the butcher, and many a

heifer, pig, and sheep have I stuck, skinned, and opened. It's a pity we were not there now! Well, I shall at least secure a warm covering and a good roast. I must attend to him now. I will soon return."

It was not long before Bav came back to the cave with the warm bear's-skin over his shoulders, and a hind-quarter of the dead animal in his arms. He spread the skin over Gustavus, and roasted the meat at the fire as well as he could.

"Eating comes first," he said, with evident satisfaction, as he cut a huge slice from the rump and devoured it, "and then sleep!"

With the last morsel still in his mouth, Bav fell down before the fire, and went to sleep, unconcerned as to any other unpleasant visitors. Yet, any one wishing to get in, would have to pass over his body before he could reach Gustavus within the cave.

The morning that followed this night of

adventure was cold and dreary. Gustavus awoke from his sleep refreshed and strengthened, but Bav was frozen almost to an icicle. In order to keep himself warm, he hung over his shoulders the skin of the bear; and, in addition to this, he encumbered himself with the other hind-quarter of the bear, greatly regretting that he must leave the remainder as a spoil for the wolves. They could travel but slowly through the deep snow, and, when they halted at noon, they had advanced scarcely four leagues. But they believed themselves safe from human pursuers, and began leisurely to prepare their dinner, the principal dish consisting of the bear-meat only half roasted before a brisk fire. Had Gustavus's situation been less critical, he could not but have smiled at seeing with what absorbing interest Bav sat before the fire, holding the meat upon a rude spit. Already had the roast begun to diffuse an odor peculiarly

agreeable to Bav's keen scent, when it
received a singular salting — a shower of
arrows that fell, quite unexpectedly, around
the two fugitives. Fortunately, most of
them missed their aim — only one of them
grazed Gustavus's cheek, and a second one
struck Bav's sore point — his head! His fur
cap, it is true, had considerably weakened the
force of the bolt, but nevertheless he opened
wide his mouth to give a terrific howl.

"Shame upon you!" cried Gustavus,
sternly. "Did you hear me scream when I
was wounded in the leg? How our enemies
would rejoice, and how eagerly would they
renew the attack, did they perceive this favorable result of their first volley. Quick!
snatch up the bear's-skin from the ground,
and wrap it around us, before the enemy can
again discharge their cross-bows." Bav
stopped short in his howl, and silently wiped
the tears from his eyes.

13   K

Scarcely had the fugitives covered themselves with the thick bear's-skin, when they
received a second volley of arrows; but this
time they fell quite harmless. The intervals
between the firing· Gustavus improved by
noting, from within his shaggy shield, the
position and number of his pursuers. Separated by a deep ravine from the spot where
Gustavus and Bav were, and at no great distance, stood the enemy—a troop of ten or
twelve horsemen—upon a high rock, from
which they had discovered the fugitives, and
had sent them, by way of greeting, the shower
of arrows.

"They are now separating," said Gustavus Vaṣa, "intending to surround us.
Three of them remain, however, to watch
us and shoot at us. Up, Bav! let us flee
yonder, where they cannot follow with their
horses!"

With the bear's-skin drawn tightly around

)

them, the twin-like pair prepared for a hasty
flight. Bav once more showed something
of his old disposition, in that he first snatched
up the spit and the roast before he obeyed
Gustavus's command to flee. He laughed
with delight as three arrows struck the bear's-
skin upon their backs, and said: "Ha!
Herre! what if I had not gotten the skin?
And the roast — it will taste good to us
yet!"

Speaking thus, Bav ran after his companion, who, thinking himself beyond the
reach of the arrows, had left the hairy shield
and hastened into a thicket. Notwithstanding the bitter cold, the fugitives were in a
perspiration when they emerged, after a time,
from the wood into the open country, where
they were surprised to find a large herd of
reindeer, who were endeavoring to find, by
the aid of their feet, a scanty nourishment
beneath the deep snow. The beautiful, use-

ful animals raised their horned heads as they heard the approach of the strangers, and looked at them inquisitively, though without fear.

Gustavus had already determined to seek a hiding-place among the friendly reindeer until he and his companion had recovered from the fatigue of their rapid flight, when the sight of a column of smoke that ascended from behind a projection of rocks suddenly changed his resolve.

The owner of the farm-house, which the fugitives soon reached, did not prove to be a very patriotic Swede; for he would not sell our hero a trained reindeer and a rough sleigh except at a very exorbitant price. To have paid the sum he demanded would have been impossible, had not Fru Mindson urged Gustavus to take Bav's blood-money — the sixty dollars. Ten of them had already been spent during their flight, and the remainder was now paid to the farmer for the reindeer and the sleigh. The latter was only intended to hold one person, but this could not separate the fugitives.

As Bav entirely filled the sleigh with his huge body, he took Gustavus on his knees before him. The latter held the reins, while Bav applied himself to the study of roast bear-meat.

The reindeer trotted off briskly, drawing the heavy load with ease over the frozen snow, in the direction which the farmer had told them led towards Norway. Gustavus had also been informed by the farmer that he had thus far been going in a zigzag way, and had really made but little progress on his journey.

They had gone perhaps a thousand steps, when suddenly four Danish horsemen sprang, with a loud cry, from the wood, and endeav-

13 *

ored to stop them. The frightened reindeer turned quickly around, and ran over the
fields so rapidly that in a few minutes they
were far beyond the cries of their pursuers.
Swift as the wind they hastened over hills,
valleys, woods, and rocks. To guide the
animal was impossible; for, at the first bound,
the reins had fallen from Gustavus's hand.
On they sped at this rapid gait for several
hours, and only then did the reindeer begin
to travel more slowly. But when Gustavus
attempted to leave the sleigh, and seize the
trailing reins, the race began anew.

It was almost night when the fugitives
reached the end of the long wood, and arrived in a valley in which stood the scattered
houses of a village. The village church was
the first building they reached. Just as
Bav cried out, clapping his hands for joy,
"Swärdsiö!" the church-bell swung, pealing
forth from the tower its mighty tones. A

sudden spring on the part of the reindeer, and the sleigh falling upon its side, tumbled its occupants to the ground. In an instant the animal and sleigh were out of sight. They had not arrived a moment too soon.

CHAPTER IX.

THE REVOLT.

THERE was great tumult in Swärdsiö. A hundred Danish soldiers had taken possession of the village, and, intoxicated by excessive draughts of liquor, had committed great outrages in the isolated farm-houses. Terribly cruel had been their treatment of Fru Mindson, who had incurred the hatred of the Danes since, by Persson's treason, it had become known that Gustavus Vasa had enjoyed her hospitality, and had found, besides, a strong defender in the person of the burly Bav.

Having first plundered the most valuable property of the widow, and then having destroyed even that which was worth but little,

they gave full scope to their cruelty, verify-
ing the proverb, " Like master, like man."

Fru Mindson sat in her yard bound fast
upon a wooden chair, her slaughtered cows
lying around her. Opposite to her stood
Rosanna, with both of her hands nailed fast
to the side of the door. The snow around
her was crimsoned with her young, fresh
blood; but, notwithstanding the terrible torture, she bore it admirably, suppressing any
cry of pain out of consideration for her
mother, whose loving heart the Danes could
so cruelly lacerate. The situation of widow
Mindson was, in truth, more painful than
even that of her daughter, as she evinced by
her heart-rending cries for mercy; which,
however, were answered by the Danes by
only fresh mockery. In the low opening
of what had once been the pigsty could be
seen the hoary, reverend head of the good
pastor, who had been placed there by the

gross whim of the rough soldiers. At a little distance was a party of Danish soldiers, armed with cross-bows and sharp bolts, who had selected Rosanna as a target. Already more than one arrow, missing its aim, remained quivering in the door. Whether a good angel had come to her rescue, or a malicious demon had hitherto guided the arrows in order to prolong her torture, seemed still undecided. There stood the maiden, having cast a long, loving look upon her fainting mother, her eyes raised devoutly to heaven, like a Christian martyr, awaiting with quiet resignation the fatal blow.

" You can't hit the mark ! " cried one of the Danes. " Give *me* the bow; I promise you I 'll hit any part of her body you name, even the lass's blue eyes."

" Keep on ringing the alarm," added the ferocious Dane, mockingly, as he placed the arrow on his bow; " we will have music to our sport."

"Hit the girl in the left eye, Broom!" cried one.

"No, Broom!" interrupted another; "strike the pastor yonder in his old preaching mouth."

Broom still stood irresolute, not knowing which suggestion to follow, when suddenly a stone, thrown with great force, struck him full on his face and stretched him on the ground. The eyes that before had followed the aim of the cross-bow, now turned in savage surprise to discover who had thrown the stone.

"Shoot down the little knave! No, take him alive, that we may torture him! After him!" Such were the exclamations of the enraged Danes. They were vented upon young Henrik, who stood upon the yard-wall with his sling in his hand, and seemed to behold with delight the success of his throw. In a moment he sprang away like a deer.

Two Danes, who ran out of the yard-gate to catch him, rushed, unfortunately for themselves, upon an unexpected obstacle — upon Bav and Gustavus, followed by a number of peasants.

"A bird to a man!" growled Bav, as, with his large knife, he clove the head of one of the Danes as coolly as if it had been a turnip or a cabbage. Nor did the other Dane, who fell into the hands of Gustavus, ever see the green grass again. So fared the soldiers in the farm-yard, whose dead bodies were soon strewn around as thickly as those of the cows and other animals they themselves had slain. Gustavus Vasa then ordered Fru Mindson to be released from the chair and Rosanna from the door. The good pastor, also, was freed from his undignified prison-house. Then all the rescued ones, Henrik among them, were left behind, under the protection of a number of armed peasants, while Gustavus and a

choice few hastened to destroy or disperse the
remainder of the Danes, who were almost as
much surprised at this sudden and unexpected uprising of the Dalecarlians as they
would have been at seeing the heavens fall.
Those of their number who were not slain fled,
at last, to a farm-house, which they turned, as
quickly as possible, into a fortress, wherein
they awaited the assault of the peasants.

The alarm-bell meantime continued to
clang, calling together, from the surround-
ing country, the people, who assembled, at
last, to the number of perhaps a thousand
men. The hastily-armed countrymen now
besieged the Danes in their place of refuge.

There was soon a cry: "Bring firebrands!
We would rather surrender our property to
the flames than endure the presence of the
cruel Danes any longer. Burn them like poi-
sonous reptiles!" On hearing this menace,
which they could readily perceive was no

14

idle threat, the Danes, who were now surrounded, lost courage. With the fumes of
the liquor their frantic insolence had also
disappeared, and a deadly fear had come
upon them. They, therefore, offered — some
sixty in all — to lay down their arms, if they
would be permitted to depart in safety.

The peasants held a council, under the
direction of Gustavus, at which they de-
liberated whether the proposal should be
accepted or rejected; and they resolved, by
his advice, to let them go. The Danes withdrew unhindered, and left behind them a
hundred effective weapons, with which were
armed as many countrymen, who formed the
first, though inconsiderable, army of Gustavus Vasa.

But the departure of the Danes by no
means checked the uprising of the Dalecarlians. In the large assembly which was
held immediately after, there was nothing

talked of but the vengeance with which the Danes, in their search for Gustavus, had threatened them. The soldiers had imprudently boasted that their King would undertake a bloody journey throughout Sweden, would erect a gallows on every farm ; and, in order to anticipate any attempt to revolt, would order an arm or a leg to be cut off from every peasant. They asserted, too, that no Swede should ever carry a sword at his side, or dare to own a cross-bow.

Gustavus understood how to improve the present disposition of the Dalecarlians. In a powerful, thrilling speech, he painted the love of freedom and the grand, heroic courage of the ancient Swedes ; he recounted the acts of cruelty and faithlessness of King Christian and his soldiers ; and, finally, he exhorted his countrymen to united resistance and a determined stand, to the death, against the foreign oppressor.

It may be doubtful, notwithstanding the
powerful influence Gustavus's speech had
made, whether it would have accomplished
the desired end, had not the following aided
his appeal — The great, strong Bav now entered the crowd, which parted to make room
for the company attending him.   These were
the old pastor and Fru Mindson, who sup-
ported and led Rosanna.   Henrik formed the
rear of the little procession, carrying in his
hand the effective sling that had struck the
first blow for liberty.

The venerable pastor bore on his face and
hands the marks of the cruel treatment he
had received from the Danes for having concealed Gustavus Vasa in his house.   So, too,
with Fru Mindson, who showed the gashes
made by the cords with which she had been
bound.   But more forcible than even the
pitiable sight of these two was the forlorn
appearance of the pale and suffering Ro-

sanna. Upon a sign from Gustavus, **Fru Mindson** loosened the bandages from the hands of her daughter.

Gustavus then took her tenderly by her arms, and, raising up her swollen, fevered hands, he cried, in a voice of emotion:

"There, my brethren! See the marks of the nails with which the cruel Danes fastened this poor child to the door. This tender body, these graceful limbs, these gentle blue eyes, this youthful, this angelic face, the Danes had selected as a target for their deadly arrows! Think you that you, *your* wives, and *your* children would fare better if those brutal Danes, each one of whom is a blood-thirsty executioner, should return to revenge themselves for those slain by us to-day! Dare we permit ourselves to be shamed by this beardless boy?" pointing to Henrik, "who alone opposed a band of soldiers, and who lifted his hand to save the life of his sister, without reflecting on the probable consequences to himself. Does not his flashing eye tell you that he is proud of his heroic deed? Do not your hearts beat quicker with the same joyful feelings, after your first victory? Well, my friends, our success to-day may be the beginning of a long series of victories by which our dear Fatherland will once more become great and free. Join with me, my brave Dalecarlians, in the common cry, 'Death to our oppressors, and triumph to our righteous cause!'"

A thousand voices echoed the cry. That same evening Gustavus set out, with a large number of the peasants, for Mora, one of the largest parishes of Dalecarlia, in order to stir up the people there to revolt against the Danes. The rumors that had preceded him of the cruelties and threats of the Danes furthered his object. On the very next day he departed, at the head of two hundred armed

Dalecarlians, to the mining-town of Falun, where he attacked the Danish governor, whom he defeated and took prisoner, together with a number of Christian's adherents. But Gustavus did not prevent his people from plundering the merchandise or stores of the Danish merchants at that place; since, by the booty thus obtained, many peasants would be induced to join his victorious countrymen. For, alas! there are now, and have always been, those among every people and nation who do right, not for its own sake, but through selfishness and greed of gain. Much that passes for patriotism is only a well-concealed selfishness. It is the prerogative, however, of a great mind, to employ even such evil-minded men in the advancement of a good cause.

Gustavus Vasa, who was chosen chieftain of Sweden in the assembly at Mora, February, 1521, taught his soldiers, after they had

beaten an army of six thousand men, under
the command of the traitor Gustav Trolle, to
manufacture better weapons, and fight according to the established rules of warfare. He in-
stituted strict discipline, and punished every
glaring transgression with death. He thus
prevented many excesses which usually mark
the progress of a great army, and by which
the peaceful inhabitants are greatly and need-
lessly injured. If so many soldiers did not
feel themselves privileged, in return for the
dangers which they incur, to violate, upon the
persons and property of their defenceless
brethren, every law of God and man, war —
that horrid offspring of hell — would be less
terrible than it is.

In May, 1521, only three months after his
first exploit against the Danish king, Gustavus ventured to make a formal declaration of
war upon him by proclamation. By a successful attack he took Wästerås, a city in West-

manland, only eleven miles from Stockholm.
After each successive victory fresh troops
flocked to his standard; and among them
were many Swedish officers who deserted
from King Christian's army and joined that
of Gustavus. He soon had around him so
many experienced soldiers, that he was ena-
bled to divide his army, and to send most of
his peasants back to their homes and their
old occupations. It was not long till the
University city of Upsala fell into Gustavus's
power; and soon there remained to be cap-
tured only Stockholm, the capital of Sweden.
Before marching thither, however, Gustavus
convened at Wadstena a Diet of the Estates of
Sweden. The Diet was numerously attended
by all classes, and among them the most distinguished noblemen. He addressed those
present with great earnestness, described the
condition of the kingdom, and called upon all
for effective aid. Touched by the noble, out-

spoken sentiments of Gustavus, all expressed a willingness to follow him to the death, and begged him at the same time to consent to become their king, since there was no one more worthy to wear the crown which King Christian had forfeited by his perfidy and cruelty.

Gustavus thanked them for the confidence shown him, but declined the proffered honor.

"Let us first drive out the Danes," he said; "it will then be time enough to choose a worthy ruler. Till then I will act as your leader, but not as your king."

CHAPTER X.

THE SACRIFICE.

IF the Swedes could not live, in the year 1523, as the Israelites once did, under their own vines and fig-trees, they nevertheless lived in much greater safety than they had two years before. With the rule of King Christian II. in Sweden ceased also the oppressions and executions; the country, in a great measure, recovered from the wounds it had received, and people of town and country could now enjoy the fruits of their labors. But the war was not ended, for the Danes still held possession of the capital, and Gustavus Vasa was now besieging it with his army. The Danish force was not sufficiently strong to hazard a pitched

battle with Gustavus, and yet could offer a
stubborn resistance behind the fortifications
of Stockholm ; and, as they were masters of
the sea, they could easily procure reinforcements and provisions from Denmark, and,
if the worst should happen, could make
good their escape.

On a certain day of May, in the above-
mentioned year, four youthful wayfarers of
almost the same age were travelling through
Sweden's blooming fields towards the capital.
They carried heavy bundles upon their backs ;
but their hearts were all the lighter, as could
readily be perceived by their merry jests.
Besides his heavy bundle, the contents of
which, by reason of its savory odor, it were
easy to guess, each of the boys carried, but-
toned to his hip, a sling and a pouch for
stones. Their resemblance to the shepherd
boy David was made complete, from the fact
that they, too, were taking cheese and savory

meat to their brethren in the camp. The names of these four Davids — Henrik, Malo, Levin, and Tauwson — are not altogether unknown to the reader; yet, he would not now recognize them at first sight, for they had grown considerably during the past two years.

"If my uncle can eat as much now as he used to," began Henrik, "the half score of cheese and the ham in my bundle will not last longer than two or three days. My mother thought so, too, and therefore declared it would not be worth the trouble of the journey. But Rosanna said that uncle would be so glad to see, by the cheese and ham, that we once more owned some cows and pigs, for which he had sent us his prize-money that he had saved with such difficulty."

"Who would have dreamed," said Malo, "that the silly Bav could ever be of any

15

account; yet now he is second only to the Administrator!"

"And if Gustavus Vasa had accepted the crown," returned Henrik, with an air of importance, "my uncle would now be second only to the King."

"What?" asked Levin; "is Bav really a captain?"

"Of course he is!" answered Henrik. "He assured us that he was always at Herre Erikson's side. And this would be something for even the most exalted in the kingdom to boast of."

"Do you remember," asked Tauwson, "that, only three years ago, Bav was so stupid as to mistake a willow-knot for a cow's head, and plunged into the lake after it?"

"Yes," added Levin, in a lower tone; "and how Henrik slung the apple at his uncle's head, and how he ran away like mad?"

"Hence," said Henrik, "as Rosanna says, he must have become more sensible. But our venerable pastor thought that war is a school in which men can, and must, learn a great deal."

"Your uncle will be astonished," said Levin, "to hear of the death of our good pastor. After his cruel treatment at the hands of the Danes, he never fully recovered his wonted strength."

"My sister Rosanna suffered much more at their hands than he," returned Henrik. "The scars can be seen on her hands even yet; and when the weather is going to change, she is apprized of it by the pains in her hands."

"But the villains received their reward!" remarked Tauwson. "To this day I envy you the lucky throw by which you struck down the dastardly Dane."

"Think you not, Tauwson," replied Henrik, "that we four might be of some use as expert slingers against the Danes? Did not the giant Goliath fall by the hand of a young slinger? What if we could return home with fame and prize-money?"

"You need only speak a good word for yourself and us to your uncle," said Malo. "If he stands so high with the Administrator, his request would not be unheeded."

This conversation would have lasted longer, had it not been interrupted by an exclamation of astonishment from Levin.

The other boys followed with their eyes the outstretched arm of Levin, when suddenly their feet became rooted to the ground. The sea, which neither of them had ever before seen, rose, with its long line of breakers, on the southern horizon, and upon the blue, foaming waves floated proudly along winged sea monsters — war-vessels crowded with snow-white canvas — which approached nearer and nearer, becoming each moment larger and more awe-inspiring.

Who then will blame the four young mountain boys for being dumb with astonishment at the sublime spectacle?

Ten three-masted vessels, whose decks were crowded with soldiers in glittering armor, and whose pennons, fluttering in the breeze, bore the standard of the free Hanse city of Lübeck, neared the coast, — a terror to the besieged, a joy to the besiegers.

Gazing intently upon the wonderful sight, the youths continued their journey in the same direction in which the vessels were sailing. Another spectacle soon again filled them with surprise and astonishment.

Imperial Rome rests upon her seven hills — Stockholm, built upon its seven islands, at the confluence of Lake Mælar and the Baltic Sea, spread itself before the bewildered gaze of the young Dalecarlians. Beside the

15 *

city proper, with the St. Nicolas Church and the Dominican cloister, was enthroned the high Ritterholm, with the royal palace and the Ritterholm Church. Farther away was the Helgrendsholm and the Norder-malm; then to the east the Schiffsholm Church, and the wharves; and, last of all, the Blasinsholm, the Ladugard landing, and the Kungsholm, studded with buildings small and large, among which the towers rose aloft into the mild May air. Besides these, were the two suburbs, separated from the other portions of the city by the south and north rivers. Around this mass of houses extended the fortifications of the city, and opposite to these, at a suitable distance, ran the earthworks of the besiegers, behind which were their tents and wooden huts.

Levin recovered his speech first.

" Just look," he said, laughing, "how wide

Tauwson opens his mouth! I believe I could throw a cheese into it."

"He wishes to swallow the whole city!" laughed Malo.

"Who could have thought that the city was so large and so beautiful!" said the astonished Henrik. "I have often secretly blamed the Administrator for lying two long years before such an old nest; but now — ha! look yonder, boys!— f-i-r-e!"

"Boom!" thundered the cannon in the ships, so that the air trembled, and the jesting Levin let fall his staff with fright.

"It's the great thunder-boxes called cannon," explained Henrik. "God have mercy upon the Danes now! Do you hear how our people shout for joy? They fire also. This is by way of greeting, as our pastor has told me from his books."

"This is a fierce noise, and I confess it does not please me," said Malo. "Hur-r-r!

how they boom. If this is sport, I wonder
what the earnest is like?"

"And now we are before Stockholm,"
thought Henrik; "but where shall we find our
friends? where are my uncle and the Administrator?"

To this question, spoken half aloud, there
came an answer which the young Dalecarlian
little expected. Two men in Swedish costume had approached the boys, unnoticed
by them, and, hearing Henrik's inquiry, one
of them broke in abruptly:

"You want to know where to find the Administrator? And what business, pray, can
you have with *him?* You don't look like one
who can approach so exalted a personage."

"I want to find my uncle," answered
Henrik, boastingly; "who is the companion
of the Administrator — nay, he is his very
shadow."

"What is your name? From what family

do you spring?" demanded the second Swede.

"I belong to the family of Mindson," returned Henrik; "and I believe it is not the worst in Dalecarlia."

"Mindson?" repeated the stranger; "I do not know the name. Is the Administrator, Gustavus Erikson, related, or only friendly, to your family?"

"Not related," said Henrik; "but friendly —yes! And yet Herre Erikson has worked upon our farm, and once received a heavy blow from my mother."

The other stranger here drew the questioner aside, and whispered to him: "Suppose we seize the boys as hostages. If Gustavus should really get the upper hand, as I now fear he will, and capture Stockholm, we might, perhaps, force him to grant us favorable conditions."

"Kätthist," replied the Swede, "do you

M

act for me.   I am almost incapable.   Would that I were a thousand miles away, or, if it were possible, back upon my farm with my wife and children.   Who would have dreamed that the helpless fugitive, Erikson, would have accomplished so much!"

"If it be as you have told us," said Kät- thist to Henrik, "follow us, and we will conduct you by the shortest route to the Administrator or to his shadow, your uncle."

"Good!" cried Henrik; "but my three companions must accompany me — this we have agreed upon."

"Who are they?   And what do they want here?" asked Kätthist, staring somewhat angrily at the three young Dalecarlians.

"Their brothers," answered Henrik, "who took an active part in expelling the Danes, and hence stand high in favor with the com- mander, are in the Swedish camp."

"Can you handle an oar?" asked Kätthist;

"for, in order to reach the Administrator quickly, we must use a boat."

"It is almost an insult to ask such a question," returned Henrik. "Do you take us for a pack of numskulls?"

"Well, then," said Kätthist, with a sinister smile, "let us be gone. Follow me as rapidly as you can."

The narrow path which Kätthist took, avoiding all the hilly ground, soon brought the little party to the sea-shore and to a little inlet, where, among the bushes, was concealed a fisherman's boat.

Kätthist took the helm, his master went to the bow of the boat, and the four young Dalecarlians together managed the oars, and that so vigorously and skilfully that the boat skimmed over the water with the greatest speed. The boys, in their eagerness, did not notice that they had passed the works of the besiegers, and that they were now approach-

ing the city and the Ritterholm itself. But
as soon as Henrik recognized, by their uni-
form, the Danes standing there upon guard,
he dropped his oar, and exclaimed: "Heaven
preserve us — there are the enemy!"

Upon this, the comrades of Henrik also
ceased rowing, and the boat rocked idly on
the waves. Then Kätthist seized an oar, his
master doing the same, and the two rowed
the boat to the shore. As they glided along,
Kätthist said, laughingly, "Enemies? Danes?
how foolishly you talk! Would the besiegers
have permitted us unmolested to row past
them? Do you not know that the Ritterholm has fallen into our hands — the hands
of the Swedes? The men you have mistaken for Danes are our own countrymen,
who have merely put on the clothes taken
from their prisoners."

Notwithstanding this speech of Kätthist,
a fearful anxiety seized the young Dalecar-

lians, and they hesitated whether to remain in the boat or endeavor to swim to the Swedish lines. By the time they had decided, it was impossible to carry out their determination, for they perceived, upon landing, that they were in the power of the Danes — into which they had been entrapped by the treacherous Persson and his servant. The Danes, however, soon satisfied themselves that they had made no great capture by entrapping the four young Dalecarlians, since it soon became evident that they were not sons of influential Swedish noblemen, but of simple peasants, and that the pretended companion of the Administrator was nothing more than a confidential menial. Nevertheless, they did not let the boys go free, but held them for any possible contingency.

As the Danish garrison in Stockholm was prevented, by the fleet from Lübeck, from receiving any reinforcements of men, money, or provisions from Denmark, there soon began to be great distress among them. Moreover, news speedily came that the people in Denmark also had revolted against Christian II., and that the King had fled from Copenhagen, a proscribed fugitive. The garrison of Stockholm, therefore, expressed a willingness to surrender, under certain conditions, to Gustavus, who, delighted at the prospect of ending the war, and freeing the capital from its enemies, consented. Terms of surrender were agreed upon, in which it was stipulated that the Danes should evacuate Stockholm within a given time, hostilities being meanwhile suspended.

On this occasion the rule that a traitor, when he is no longer needed, can hope for no consideration for himself, was confirmed. Favorable as were the terms which the Danes could make for themselves by the stipulations agreed upon, all those Swedes who had assisted the Danish cause by deed, word, or counsel were excluded from the provisions of the treaty. Among these was the traitor Persson, who now began to fear for his life. In order to leave no means untried to escape the threatening destruction, he, by the advice of Kätthist, improved the seemingly favorable circumstance of having in his power Henrik and his companions.

A little while before the termination of the truce granted the Danes, Bav, in full military dress, entered the tent of the Administrator, carrying in his hand a letter.

"There's a young fellow outside, Herre," he began, "whose name is Malo. He comes from my village, and says he is an old acquaintance. But I cannot remember all the little fellows who have grown up since I left. He handed me this letter, and said it came from Henrik, my nephew. But it cannot be true, for where could he have learned to write. Malo has told me many other wonderful things, all of which may be lies. Read it, Herre, for, as you know, I cannot."

Gustavus took the letter, and smiled as he read the address, "*To my uncle Bav, who is second only to the Administrator.*" He unfolded it, and read:

"DEAR UNCLE:—If you wish to prevent me and the other three—Levin, Malo, and Tauwson—from being strangled, beg your good friend, Gustavus Vasa, to pardon Herre Persson, and permit him to return to his wife and children. He promises never to do wrong again. If Herre Gustavus consents, let him accompany Malo, who will conduct him to a place where Herre Persson awaits him, to hear his pardon from Gustavus's own mouth and before witnesses. Should Malo not return, I will be cruelly tortured, and then murdered. How we came here, and how all this has come to pass, Malo will tell you.

Your brother's child,

HENRIK MINDSON."

"This is the story of Shimei," said Gustavus Vasa, earnestly.

"And who was he?" asked Bav. "I don't know him."

"That I may well believe," returned Gustavus. "He lived before your time, and was the Israelite who cursed and threw stones at King David when fleeing before his rebellious son, but was the first to fall beseechingly at his feet when the King returned victorious. What do you advise me to do, Bav?"

"*I* advise you, Herre?" cried Bav. "Oh, Herre! you mock me!"

"You are right—you dare not counsel me in this—it concerns your own flesh and blood," said Gustavus, thoughtfully. "This miserable Persson who wanted to sell me to the Danes—ha! how would it be with my Fatherland now had he succeeded? And yet, Gustavus, art thou more than a weak instrument in the hands of the Almighty,

16 *

who could easily have freed thy Fatherland without thee? Compelled to wander around for two years, oppressed by the burden of a guilty conscience, shunning wife and children and home, has not the wretched traitor been chastened enough already? In punishing the husband and father, would I not also inflict punishment upon his innocent wife and children? Dare I hesitate when the life of a near relative of a faithful friend and the preserver of *my* life is at stake? Come, Bav, follow me!"

Bav obeyed the command, and stalked behind his master, accompanied by Malo and a few nobles, to the appointed place between the works of the besiegers and the fortifications of Stockholm. Having arrived upon the spot, Malo pointed to an opening in the breastworks, where stood the traitor Persson, trembling between hope and fear. Behind him could be seen the villanous countenance of Kätthist.

Gustavus turned his sincere and noble countenance upon that of the traitor, raised his right hand solemnly, and said, in a loud voice: "I promise, before Almighty God and these witnesses, that I will take no revenge on you, Persson, for the past; but on condition —"

Simultaneously with the snapping of a distant cross-bow, Bav's lips uttered a cry of terror; and at the same instant, Gustavus Vasa, thrust aside by the powerful arm of his attendant, was hurled to the ground. Then Bav, dashing forward, threw out his arms, as if to protect his loved master, and stood like a tower. A heavy arrow sped whizzing through the air, and then buried itself deep in Bav's broad, open breast.

With a groan he fell to the earth.

So dastardly an act was naturally followed by a tumult as great as it was general. Upon the cry, "Treason! Murder! Revenge!"

the crowds of Swedes who hastened thither
would at once have scaled the ramparts and
taken bloody vengeance upon the Danes, but
Gustavus restrained the infuriated men. The
few Danes that remained, fearing for their
lives, straightway seized Persson and Kätthist, and delivered them both to Gustavus
Vasa.

The former solemnly asserted his innocence of the cowardly act; and the latter,
himself struggling with death, confirmed the
statement, but denied that he had aimed at
Gustavus Vasa.   He said that he had wished
to revenge himself on Bav alone for the
rough treatment he had received from him
before the servants and domestics at Persson's.

Immediately after his deed, the assassin
had thrust his dagger into his own breast,
that he might not fall alive into the hands of
the executioner.

"Whether the murderer's story be true or false, I know not," said Gustavus; "but this I know full well — the deadly weapon would have **struck me** had not **the** faithful Bav become the victim in my stead."

Turning to his mortally wounded companion, he **said** tenderly: "Oh, **my** preserver from many dangers, **how I** thank thee **for** thy sacrifice! Wouldst thou die *now*, when such a glorious future awaits our Fatherland? No, thou must — thou wilt — live long, to enjoy the **rich** fruits of our hard struggle!"

But Bav slowly shook his faithful head. "Believe me, Herre," he murmured, **in a** feeble voice, "Persson's servant was no bad shot. For such a wound, this world knows no cure. And **yet, I do** not grieve. My wounded breast oppresses me, but my heart is all the lighter. I have shed innocent blood, and mine must flow now. This is **a** just atonement. Only one word more —"

A stream of blood that gushed from his pale lips interrupted his speech, and the long swoon that succeeded deprived him of consciousness. He was borne carefully to the camp, and given into the charge of a skilful surgeon.

CHAPTER XI.

FORGIVENESS AND DEATH.

IN the spacious hall of the royal palace in Stockholm sat Gustavus Vasa, surrounded by the Deputies and Estates of the kingdom. After the full deliverance of his country from the Danes, he had desired to resign his office of the Administratorship, but had been urged by the whole Assembly to accept the crown.

To this request he answered:

"A king is the most unhappy of men. Do as he may, he can never rule to please all. Our Fatherland still needs many and great sacrifices, and to ask them from the people would be the King's first duty. I am neither vain nor proud, that I should strive to

obtain the splendor of a crown, which often
chills and crushes the head that wears it.
Yes, my friends, I do not feel myself able to
heal the land of the many wounds from
which it still bleeds. Surely you can find
among you one more worthy than I, a poor
soldier, who was able to offer resistance to
the Danes only by the help of you brave,
intrepid Swedes."

At this declaration, most of those present
burst into tears; many fell upon their knees,
and besought the Administrator not to withdraw his services from his Fatherland at this
time. Even the Papal ambassador exhorted
the Deputies not to cease imploring him.
This repeated, earnest solicitation Gustavus
could no longer resist. He consented; and,
full of heartfelt joy, they all took the oath
of allegiance. The new King, on the other
hand, swore that he would rule according to
the laws of the land.

"I pray God," he said, "to give me the wisdom that He gave to Solomon, to rule my people justly. Even the wisest of men may err, and mistakes may cling to the crown and sceptre as well as to the sword. I, too, may sometimes fail in the performance of my duty. At such times I shall thank the just man who will tell me the honest truth in a becoming manner; and the flatterer, who calls wrong right, I will despise. But one thing more, my countrymen: I beg of you an unreserved confidence, which, next to our holy religion, is the firmest support of the throne as well as of the happiness of the people."

The shout that followed these royal words had scarcely died away, before several petitioners were announced to the new-crowned King.

"Behold, my friends," said Gustavus Vasa, to the assembly, smiling, "already, in the first hour of my new dignity, my trouble

17   N

begins. How many petitions will henceforth be brought to my ears which it will be impossible for me to grant! Yet I dare not refuse an audience to the petitioners that come to me even in this glorious hour. Let them advance."

Hereupon a woman approached from the wide circle, leading by each hand a child. She walked in silence to the throne of the King; in silence she knelt with her children before him; tears glistened in her eyes, and a heavy sigh escaped her lips.

"What is thy wish, my good woman?" asked the King, kindly; "speak boldly!"

"I am the wife of Persson — these are his children!" replied the trembling woman. "Oh, King, extend to our husband and father your royal favor. Forgive him his guilt."

"This," returned Gustavus Vasa, "is much to ask. His first treason, like all transgression, has been followed by a series of crimes. His treachery has caused me to mourn the loss of the most faithful of servants — my deliverer from numerous perils. For never would the wretched assassin have dared to lay his hand on me, or my companion, had not thy husband been to him a wicked example. Nevertheless, I have already assured him of pardon; and what the Administrator has promised, the King will perform. Arise, good woman, and await thy husband."

At a sign from the King, Persson was brought in. He presented a sad picture of a guilty wretch, upon whom all present looked with contempt, loathing, and indignation.

Pale, trembling, and with downcast eyes, Persson awaited his fate.

" Persson," said the King, "thou art free! Yes, go and be happy, if thou canst be happy after thy sins. But I counsel thee —

hide thyself and thy shame in the solitary
mountain retreat, whence thou didst go to
betray him who is now thy King. To thy
noble wife, and these, thy children, thou
owest thy present pardon — be thankful,
therefore, and be a good husband and father.
Go in peace." Then turning to the wife,
he added: "To thee and thy children, I
shall ever be a faithful friend. I am thy
debtor."

Once more the noble woman knelt in
silence at the feet of the King, and then,
with her husband and children, she tottered
towards the door. But, before she had left
the hall, she was met by a woman dressed in
deep mourning, who stood still, as she saw
the children, wrung her hands in silent woe,
and then cried out, despairingly: "*My* children were like these! My loved, my innocent children!"

She then pressed them tenderly to her

heart, and covered the astonished little ones with countless kisses.

"Who is she?" passed from mouth to mouth.

"Who art thou?" asked the King. "What is thy petition?"

"Has grief so changed me," asked the woman, throwing back from her sorrowful, wasted features the widow's veil, "that no one can recognize me? I am Anna Ribbing, the unhappiest of mothers! What do I wish from you? I no longer know. The sight of these two children has driven all other thoughts from my mind; yes, O King, give me back my children, and I will bless you through all eternity."

"This is a request," said the King to the assembly, "to grant which is beyond human power. Woman! am I then a God, who can bring to life the dead? And even if I were able to do so, I would yet forbear to exercise

17 *

the power. Does selfishness make thee so
cruel towards thy children that thou canst
wish them to return to this world of sorrow
from the enjoyment of heaven? Would they
not have to pass, sooner or later, again
through the agony of death? We should
live, not for earth, but for heaven. Thither
turn thy looks and thy desires. Mark what
I have yet to say to thee. As Jesus Christ
has become the corner-stone of our holy religion, so have thy murdered children become
the corner-stone of our deliverance from the
Danish yoke. Their execution roused the
indolent and enslaved Swedes to revolt
against the foreign tyrant. Did thy children
still live, we, and all the thousands of Sweden's children, would yet be under the threatening sword of King Christian — not sure of
our lives for a day. Yes, madam, from the
innocent blood of thy dear children has
sprung the Liberty Tree of Sweden. Even

the blood-money received for the deed has, in my hands, become a blessing. And, above all, the murder of thy children has wrought a wondrous miracle — has made a new man of a weak-minded, silly peasant, to the great good of his fellow-man. If I have been an instrument, in God's hands, of doing my country some service, Sweden, nevertheless, owes much to this man, without whose assistance I would surely have fallen (and that, too, more than once) into the hands of the Danes. And now one word more: wouldst thou cherish anger towards the unwitting instrument who, by the command of the King, was the executioner of thy youngest child? Art thou a Christian? Oh! then, imitate the example of Him who, even upon the cross, prayed for His murderers. Not without a purpose, as thou wilt soon discover, has God directed thy steps hither."

The King then whispered a few words to

one of the Swedes standing near by, who at
once hastily left the apartment. All looked
with intense interest for what should follow.

The door of the hall soon opened, and the
four youthful Dalecarlians, Henrik, Malo,
Levin, and Tauwson, slowly entered, carrying
a litter, which they set down, in silent rev-
erence, before the King. It may easily be
guessed who lay upon the bed; but it would
have been almost impossible to recognize in
those attenuated lineaments the giant Bav, the
former Hercules. The expression was changed
by the skeleton hand of Death. Yet he
seemed to be as tall as ever — nay, taller;
but his broad, full breast had become nar-
rowed and sunken; a white transparent hue
covered the once round, ruddy face, which
now bore upon each cheek a bright crimson
spot. His forehead was dignified with the
seal of death, and his beautiful, honest blue
eyes shone deep in their sockets. His lips

were pale and bloodless, so that the lines of his mouth could scarcely be distinguished; and his big hands were fleshless bones covered with shrivelled skin. The giant Bav, once a terror to his enemies, had become, as must we all, a withered leaf, which the hand of Death prepares to shake from the autumn tree.

As the King approached the litter, a tender smile illumined the wan features of the dying man, and the wasted right hand slowly raised itself from the couch. The King took it between his own, and pressed it affectionately to his breast. Then, turning to the widow Ribbing, he spoke:

"Behold, madam, the unwitting instrument of the death of your youngest son. Notwithstanding he committed the act ignorantly, yet he has bitterly repented it, and has sought to atone for it by a life of self-denial and fidelity. Fru Ribbing, if thy daily

prayer, 'Our Father which art in heaven,' is
no mere mockery, oh then forgive this *thy*
debtor, that God may also forgive thee!
Shall this poor man go without a kindly
greeting from thee to thy sainted children?"

The widow, who had been so cruelly deprived of her children, then approached the
dying Bav. She laid her hand upon his
damp forehead, and said, solemnly: "From
my heart I forgive thee; may our Lord forgive thee!"

"I hope so," whispered Bav, in a feeble
voice; "for the sake of my crucified Saviour.
Yes, I *know* it — for do you not see, oh,
mother — there," pointing with his raised
hand, "do you not see your little boy with
the flaxen locks! He is not angry with me
now! He smiles so pleasantly — he beckons
to me — he stretches his hands towards me —
I come, sweet child, I come —"

His hand dropped heavily upon the couch;

his head fell back upon the pillow. One more deep respiration, and the angel of Death stamped a radiant smile upon the mild, glorified features. Thus died the peasant Bav.

"Oh take me with you!" sobbed Fru Ribbing, as she knelt beside the litter. The boy Henrik kissed the cold hand of his uncle, and wept bitterly, while the other youths gazed regretfully upon the lifeless body.

The King claimed the privilege of closing the eyes of the dead, saying, as he did so, with words almost choked by emotion, "I have become richer by a crown — poorer by the loss of a friend. God's peace be over and about thee, my preserver!"

As Gustavus turned aside to conceal his emotion and his tears, the people, honoring the noble grief of their King, silently withdrew from the hall.

CHAPTER XII.

REWARD AND PUNISHMENT.

I HOPE no harm has happened to Henrik," said Fru Mindson, anxiously, to her daughter. "He should have been home before this. I wish I had not let the restless fellow go! All the work of the farm now devolves upon us two! Owing to the war, farm hands are hard to get, and still harder to keep. Nor is it easy to procure maid-servants either, for they prefer to work where there are men to help them. Bav is no longer with us — though he ate us poor, rather than helped us; and now Henrik is gone, too! True, there is little to do in the stable, but in the field all the more. The horses are gone, and had not brother Bav

204

remembered us, we would have no cows or pigs, either.   But — Rosanna! what's that? Hark!"

"Trumpets and shouting!" exclaimed Rosanna, turning pale, for, since the time when she had been so cruelly treated by the Danes, she had become exceedingly timid.

"Alas! the Danish troopers cannot be coming again?" cried Fru Mindson, excitedly.

Mother and daughter listened intently.

"This is no battle-cry or shriek of woe," said the former, after a pause, somewhat composed.

"Just look, mother, what is coming!" exclaimed the daughter.

Four handsomely dressed trumpeters, their glittering trumpets hung with sky-blue ribbons, came riding along the village road, their broad-brimmed hats and their left breasts decorated with garlands of bright

18

flowers; and they blew so lustily into the
bright metal that it almost seemed as though
their full, rosy cheeks must burst. A little
flock of snow-white sheep, preceded by a
ram, to whose wide, branching horns was
fastened a little silver bell by a blue ribbon,
followed the trumpeters. The name of the
young shepherd who drove the sheep with a
white crook, also decorated with blue ribbons, was Malo, who was dressed in new
clothes from head to foot. Then came three
goats with as many kids, who joined their
bleating with that of the sheep. These were
led by Levin, who wore a wreath upon his
hat and breast, as did the rest. It had fallen
to Tauwson's lot to be the driver of six half-
grown swine, which gave him no little trouble,
as they were continually falling out of line.
But the poor, perspiring fellow was entirely
forgotten on the appearance of seven sleek,
well-fed cows, that resembled the seven fat

kine of King Pharaoh, from the neck of the
foremost of which, whose color was a beautiful brown, hung a silver bell, whose clear
sound could be heard at a great distance.
As Henrik's blooming face appeared behind
these well-favored seven, Fru Mindson's
astonishment turned to joy, which she expressed in a loud call that was answered on
the part of Henrik by a merry nod. The foremost of the horsemen that led the rear guard
of this motley company was distinguished
alike by his rich dress and his dignified
bearing. The trumpeters, meantime, rode
straight to the spot where Fru Mindson and
her daughter were standing; and the latter
hastened to open the gate, in which office
she was assisted by the peasantry, who
flocked in advance of the procession. And
lo! the trumpeters, the sheep, the goats, the
cows, the pigs, the herd-boys, the horsemen,
and all the people entered the farm-yard of

the astounded widow, who was forced back
farther and farther by the throng. The
present which the homeward-bound Jacob
sent to his brother Esau may have looked
not unlike this. And, in truth, these animals
were intended as a present, and that to Fru
Mindson. For amidst the shouts of the
people, "God save the King! Long live
our King!" Gustavus Vasa himself dis-
mounted from his horse, and advancing to
Fru Mindson, who, with her daughter, had
fallen on her knees before him, said kindly :

"Arise, good woman, it becomes thee not
to kneel. Was I not once thy servant, and
wert thou not my kind mistress? Could I
have a more sacred duty to perform, after the
enemy had been driven out, than to repay a
debt of gratitude? True, Sweden is now
poor, and her King, too, is poor; but this must
not prevent him from rewarding, according to his ability, those who have befriended

him. This little herd of animals, however, is not a present from thy King but the bequest of thy brother-in-law, who died for me. May God reward him for his fidelity. And just here it occurs to me that thou once didst strike thy King a weighty blow upon the shoulder, which, before I say more, I must repay with interest. Kneel, good woman, and," he added with a smile, " do not be too greatly alarmed."

For Fru Mindson trembled like an aspen leaf, and was pale as death. And, as she fell upon her knees, the King drew his glittering sword, and, gently striking her three times upon the shoulder with the flat of the blade, said, solemnly: " I hereby create thee, Eva Mindson, a baroness of Sweden, and will that your descendants be barons and baronesses. At the same time, I raise thy property to the rank of a freehold estate, subject henceforth to no tax, imposts, or rents. I add to it,

18 *   O

moreover, ten acres of meadow land that border upon it, which hitherto have belonged to the crown, so that the bequest of your brother-in-law may not want for pasture."

When the King had spoken these royal words, he raised Fru Mindson from her knees, and graciously pressed her hand. He then requested Rosanna to show him the scars on her hands; and, as he looked, he took occasion to put on the finger of the blushing girl a heavy gold ring, and around her snow-white neck he hung a massive golden chain, for he knew how the hearts of womankind, and especially of young girls, are set upon glittering trinkets. One of the attendants of the King — the treasurer — quietly placed upon the old deal table a sealed bag of hard Swedish dollars — the number of which was not marked on the outside, but it was more than equal to the sixty dollars — the blood-money which Fru Mindson had given to the fugitive, Gustavus Erikson — with interest compounded. Fru Mindson, amidst tears of joy and gratitude, had hardly secured the sheep, goats, pigs, and cows in the stalls, when she was astonished anew to see that the four trumpeters had changed from horsemen to footmen, and that their spirited horses now neighed and stamped in Fru Mindson's own stable, being intended by the King to cultivate the land of the new freehold : " How kind and how condescending is our King ! " shouted the people.

The King now left the farm-yard and all the people with him. So, too, Fru Mindson and her two children, Rosanna and Henrik, who now told his mother about the splendid burial of his uncle Bav, and the costly monument erected to his memory in Stockholm. Soon they arrived in the centre of the village, where stood a flower - decked vehicle drawn by four horses, the contents of which were as wonderful as they were costly, and awakened new and still greater astonishment. A large, shining crown rested upon the variegated flowers more becomingly than upon the most magnificent velvet cushion. The King led the way, followed by the carriage bearing the crown, and the crowd of people repaired to the churchyard of Swärdsiö. Having arrived there, Gustavus Vasa asked to be shown the grave of the sainted pastor, who had concealed him for eight days, and had then recommended him to his colleague at Rättwick. As he approached the modest grave, the King uncovered his head, and all the people with him. And kneeling, as did the people, he uttered a prayer of praise and thanksgiving for the honored dead, and the multitude cried devoutly, "Amen! Amen!"

"See," said the peasants, deeply touched by the scene, "how pious is our King!"

The King then ordered the golden crown to be placed upon the tower of the church, that its lustre might proclaim far over the land the praise of the good pastor.

And again the people exclaimed joyfully: "What a grateful King is ours!"

History tells us that the King really travelled the country over, in order to thank those who had helped him. And thus it comes to pass that the Swedish people are grateful, too; and, among other relics, they preserve intact to this day — out of regard for the memory of Gustavus Vasa — the barn in which he thrashed, even though awkwardly, as a hired servant.

The Swedish people believed that, from the virtue of gratitude possessed by their King, they could infer the existence in him of other virtues; and in this they were not deceived. Kings and other great personages are not always thus grateful for good services rendered them. Often, and very soon, have they forgotten their promises so readily made to their deliverers in the hour of danger, of which we have an example in the chief butler of King Pharaoh. Sweden grew rapidly and became powerful under Gustavus Vasa's rule, and has increased in size and importance up to the present time.

And King Christian II., what has become of *him?*

This wicked monarch, after he had practised every species of cruelty upon the Swedes, began to treat his own people in the same manner. They were at last obliged to do as the Swedes had done — they drove away the tyrant, and elected in his place Frederick, Duke of Holstein, the introducer of the Lutheran Reformation into Denmark. Christian, it is true, opposed the election, and endeavored to depose the new king by force of arms, and for this purpose had assembled an army; but his money was soon spent, and, as a tyrant is served only for pay, his soldiers deserted, leaving the King in the power of his enemy, who took him captive, and confined him in an old castle, where he was separated from his wife and daughters for a number of long, weary years.

Here he had time and opportunity to repent. But as Christian had never given himself much concern about religion, this sole source of comfort and consolation was closed to him. Except the soldiers who guarded him, Christian, who once had been surrounded by a host of venal courtiers and flatterers, saw no one in his solitude save an ugly old Norwegian dwarf, who, like nearly all such creatures, vented his rage at his deformity by bitter rancor against all better favored men; nor did he spare even the dethroned King.

"Hand me a glass of Burgundy, Teebs,"

said Christian to his little servant, one after-
noon in the autumn of 1560. The dwarf
left the room, and returned with a glass of
water, which, with a look of spiteful delight,
he placed before the King.

"This, old man," he said, "is better for
you than the fiery Burgundy, which only
inflames your blood and turns your head."

As the exasperated King seized the glass
to throw it at the ill-shaped head of his
malicious tormentor, Teebs sprang mockingly away, and bolted in the King's face the
door of the room into which he fled. Christian, in his rage, shattered the glass to pieces
against the door, and he cried, in his im-
potent wrath : "Oh, if I had only a sword that
I might stab this noxious worm !"

"Or your quondam executioner," jeered
the dwarf through the key-hole, "that you
might do with me as you did with the innocent little Ribbings! Aha, I have you there."

"Wretch!" stammered Christian, as he left the door. "Must you forever conjure up the bloody shadows which I once thought I had banished from my memory?"

For a long time Christian paced his chamber to and fro, absorbed in thought. At last he started at the sound of his own footsteps, shuddered, and shrunk towards the bolted door.

"I am no longer angry with you, Teebs," he said, in tones that now meant to be conciliatory.

"But I am angry with you!" returned the ugly dwarf.

"Come in, good Teebs," added Christian, earnestly.

"I will not!" answered the dwarf, stubbornly.

"Your *King* beseeches you; do you hear, Teebs, your *King?*"

"A pretty king!" sneered the dwarf; "with-

19

out land or people, without crown or sceptre, without servants or soldiers!"

Christian clinched his fists again, but only for a few seconds. His rage was mastered by his fears.

"*Do* come in, Teebs! I will not be un — unjust to you again."

"You have promised me this a hundred times before, and have never kept your word," replied the dwarf. "You have never kept your word — not even your *oath* when confirmed by the Holy Sacrament!"

At this Christian gnashed his teeth fiercely, and his wrinkled face became distorted.

With a fierce oath he exclaimed, in an undertone: "What ignominy! and yet I cannot be revenged!"

For a while he stood irresolute, struggling with himself; at last he said, in an imploring voice:

"Will you not grant my wish upon *any* condition?"

"First pick up from the floor the pieces of glass," answered Teebs; "perhaps I may then be persuaded. But you must pick them *all* up," he added, authoritatively.

And the whilom tyrant bent his crooked back and his stiffened knees, and, obedient to the command of the churlish dwarf, picked up the pieces of glass.

"Are you done yet?" asked the dwarf, impatiently.

"Yes, good Teebs," replied the exhausted King. The door opened, and the dwarf entered the room. The monarch seated himself upon an arm-chair, and gazed listlessly through the grated window.

"Strike a light," begged Christian, anxiously. "Do you not see, Teebs, how long the shadows are getting?"

"Why?" asked the dwarf, peevishly: "it's

light enough yet for *your* work. Or perhaps you see spectres in the twilight?"

"*Do* grant me this favor, Teebs," implored Christian; "for I shall die before very long."

The dwarf laughed maliciously. "You have been promising me this for a long time," he said; "and even in this you are a liar. It would, indeed, be the best thing for you and for me, for your life is a burden to yourself and to all. If I could only believe that you were speaking the truth, I would light all the candles in the castle."

"Oh *do*, Teebs!" begged Christian. "Do! do! my heart has all at once grown so heavy!"

"It's only dissimulation," said Teebs to himself; but he went for candles, and lighted them.

The King was seated in his arm-chair; he watched the dwarf closely as he arranged the candles around the room.

"Well, does it please you, old man?" asked Teebs.

"Come here," begged Christian, breathing heavily; "stand before me — so! — a little to the right — no — more to the left — *so that I cannot see them.*"

"What is it you see?" croaked the dwarf; "the BLOOD-BATH at Stockholm, or THE TWO LITTLE RIBBINGS?"

Christian made no reply to the question of his tormentor. His eyes closed, then opened — a cold sweat stood upon his forehead, and the clammy, attenuated hand, which he extended out so beseechingly, touched the clothes of the dwarf, who stood near him.

"Don't soil my good clothes," laughed the dwarf; "my mother will scold me."

Christian's head sunk upon his panting breast, raised itself once more, and for the last time; his eye already glazed shone once more with a deadly fire; his right hand was

19 *

lifted once again as if to strike a furious blow.

Then the angel of death smote him that he died. He fell back in his chair stiff and lifeless.

The dwarf approached, in each hand a burning candle, which he held close to the face of the King.

"Thank God!" he cried, "he is really dead, and I am free!"

He turned his back upon the royal corpse, extinguished the lights, and left the room, to announce to the guards the death of the King.

Thus died King Christian, upon whom history has stamped the unenviable titles of "TYRANT," "The Nero of the North," "Christian the Angry."

Who would not rather die the death of the simple, faithful, peasant Bav, than that of the wicked King?—the one honored and trusting in his SAVIOUR; the other despised and without Hope.

The lives, too, of the perjured usurper and of the patriotic Erikson afford a contrast that it would be well for the reader to ponder. The name of King Christian II. is remembered with obloquy; that of Gustavus Vasa is the boast of every true-hearted Swede.

HISTORIC SKETCHES

OF THE

LIFE AND TIMES

OF

GUSTAVUS VASA,

BY

REV. PROF. A. L. GUSS, A. M.

GUSTAVUS VASA.

. Harper & Bros.' Edition of "Denmark, Sweden, and Norway."

HISTORIC AND REFLECTIVE
SKETCHES

SUGGESTED BY THE PERUSAL OF THIS NARRATIVE.

I T will be perfectly natural for those who have read this story, and are not familiar with the history of Sweden, to wish to know something more of the country and the men introduced to the reader in this narrative. The following facts of history have, therefore, been collected and woven together for the benefit of those who cannot study a more extended account. In doing so, the writer has not thought it necessary to formally quote the words, or give the names of the authors from whom these facts were gathered.

Those countries now known as Sweden, Denmark, and Norway were formerly known as Scandinavia ; and emigrants to America from those countries are even yet often called Scandinavians.

The people are doubtless of German or Gothic origin. Before them, and beyond them, lived the Finns, whose limits cannot now be determined, but who were driven back by the superior power of the Germans. These northern races existed, like our North American Indians, for many centuries in a state of barbarism, divided into tribes, and separated from each other and from the rest of the world. They lived in a state of natural liberty, and nearly without law or organized government. Though various writers have mentioned them, and faint glimpses may be caught of the character of the people, yet it would be folly in any writer to attempt to pen a connected history of them prior to the tenth century. And it is a strange fact, that the earliest and most authentic annals of their history come from Iceland, where they had been preserved, as classics, through the dark ages, by learned men who had emigrated thither, as our forefathers came to America, to enjoy freedom.

Some historians speak of the early history of Scandinavia as *uninteresting;* but a country that sent out the Northmen to people Iceland, Greenland, and even to discover America near 500

years before the time of Columbus, and could
send forth such vast hordes of Goths and Sea-
kings as to fill the history of Europe, for 200
years, with accounts of their ravages; though its
history may be obscure and void of consistency;
yet it can never be said to be *uninteresting* to
any one wishing to acquaint himself with the
great events of the past, which have done so
much to shape the present. The past history
of Scandinavia has influenced the present condition of all Europe.

The early history of Sweden is certainly
obscure. No certain knowledge of its inhabitants, or their origin, is afforded by history until
after the period of its occupation by the Goths.
These fierce and warlike people, emigrating from
the north of Persia at some period which cannot
now be fixed, spread themselves over Scandinavia. Respecting Sweden, little was known in
southern Europe until the bold incursions of the
Northmen, and the introduction of Christianity
about the year 1000, attracted the attention of
the civilized world.

Previous to this time, Sweden was known only
by fabulous reports concerning it. The religion

was Pagan, and the principal deity was Odin or Wodin, a personage who settled in the North, and died B. C. 70. The Christian religion was not fully established until about half a century after its introduction under Olaf III. It was then generally diffused by the exertions of Ingi, surnamed the Pious. The Gothic race did not mix with any other people, and the population of the lower part of Sweden is, therefore, purely Gothic. The northern part is inhabited by a remnant of the Finnish tribes, who are supposed to have been the original inhabitants.

The year 1387 introduces a better known and more important era in Swedish history. At this time Sweden, Norway, and Denmark were distinct kingdoms. It marks an epoch of great change in the language and literature of the North. Still, the Swedes were behind their neighbors in the adjoining kingdoms. Even those great changes in policy and manners which, at this period, began among most nations, did not take place in Sweden till near the middle of the 16th century. Her whole history prior to that time furnishes only a wretched detail of civil wars, insurrections, and revolu-

tions, arising principally from the jealousies sub-
sisting between the kings, and the nobles, and the
people ; the one party striving to augment their
power, and the others to maintain their independence.   In fact, the fruits of literature and
science did not begin to ripen in those ungenial
climes until the doctrines of Luther had opened
the eyes of men to the delusions under which
they had been so long held in intellectual thraldom.   It was during the reign of Gustavus Vasa,
the patron of letters and commerce, that the
Swedes first acquired a taste for knowledge, and
began to cultivate the arts of peaceful improve-
ment.   The Reformation totally cut off the
source of those disturbances which the wealth,
pride, and ambition of the Romish prelates had
formerly created.

At the time spoken of above, Margaret, daughter of Valdemar, King of Denmark, and widow
of Hakon VI., King of Norway, was, by the death
of her father and son, made ruler of both these
kingdoms.   She compelled Albert, Duke of
Mecklenberg, reigning King of Sweden, to give
up his crown ; and then, by the famous treaty
of Calmar in 1397, the three northern kingdoms

20 *

were united under one head.   It was agreed that
they should be forever governed by one sovereign, to be chosen successively from each kingdom, who should have his election confirmed by
the other two ; that each nation was to retain its
own laws, customs, and privileges ; and that the
natives of one kingdom should not be advanced
to offices of trust or emolument in the other.

The vigor of Margaret's administration, and
her military exploits, have rendered her name
illustrious as "the Semiramis of the North."
The wisdom and sagacity of Margaret's policy
restrained, in some degree, the jealousy and
hatred that existed between the Swedes and the
Danes.   The fiery nature of the Swedes could
not well stand the unrestrained insolence of the
Danes under a union imposed upon them by
force of arms.   Margaret died in 1412, having
reigned in Denmark thirty-seven years.   She was
celebrated as a heroine by the Danes, and exalted
to a high pitch of greatness ; but she was far from
being endeared to the people of Sweden, whom
she treated as a conquered rather than a con-
federate nation.   This wounded the pride of the
brave and ancient nobility in the tenderest point.

They saw foreigners monopolize the offices and occupy the strongholds of the kingdom. Even had the Union of Calmar been conceived in more foresight and wisdom than it was, it must, under such circumstances, have failed to reconcile the long-standing jealousies and bitter rivalries.

Margaret was succeeded by Erik, under whom, in 1448, the Swedes revolted; and there followed a long series of bloody and barbarous wars, in which the Swedes were sometimes victorious and then again subjugated, until finally Christian II., King of Denmark, reduced them effectually to the condition of a conquered people.

Sten Sture had been chosen regent and administrator by the Swedes at the time of the revolt from Christian I. His son succeeded to the regency, but was opposed by Gustavus Trolle, Archbishop of Upsal and primate of Sweden, whom Christian II. had bought over to his interest. Having been disgraced and deprived of his bishopric by the diet, Trolle instigated Pope Leo X. to issue a bull of excommunication against the regent and all his supporters, the execution of which was committed to the care of Christian

II., who performed it in a manner that has gained for him in history the title of "the Nero of the North." Availing himself of this pretext, the misnamed king invaded Sweden, and, having been defeated in battle, he endeavored to attain by fraud, perfidy, and stratagem what he failed to perform by military force. He offered to go in person to Stockholm, and confer with the regent Sture, in regard to terms of peace, provided six hostages, whom he should name, were given for his safety. He selected Gustavus Erikson, a descendant of an illustrious family that had for over 200 years taken an active part in public affairs, as one of the hostages, with five other noblemen, who, by the consent of the Senate, were placed on board the Danish fleet. The faithless Christian, finding that he had them in his power, ordered them to be disarmed, arrested, and taken to Copenhagen, threatening their death as heretics and rebels unless the Swedes would restore the primate Trolle, and re-establish the Union of Calmar. Gustavus was committed to the care of a noble named Banner, who agreed to confine him in his castle of Callundborg, in Jutland, or pay a penalty of 6000 florins in case of his escape. The other prisoners were confined in different fortresses, and treated with the greatest severity.

The following year, 1520, Christian returned to Sweden with an immense army, gathered from every country of Europe. The celebrated Paracelsus served as a surgeon in this army. The invaders ravaged the country, killed the regent Sten Sture in an ambuscade, and, taking advantage of the indecision of the Swedish Senate in the selection of a successor, they called a diet at Upsala, where the primate Trolle expatiated on the wretchedness the nation had brought upon itself by opposing the just claims of Christian to the Swedish crown. His arguments were successful, and a treaty of amnesty and oblivion was entered into by the parties. Christina, widow of Sten Sture, fled to Stockholm, and for a time, by her example and patriotism, resisted the enemy, but was forced, at last, by famine to surrender. Trolle now resumed his functions as Archbishop of Upsal, and primate; and, in the city of Stockholm, publicly transferred the crown of Sweden to the head of the perfidious Dane.

Christian promised a general amnesty, and
swore on the altar of God, in the cathedral of
Stockholm, not to rule with the severity of a conqueror, but with the lenity of a father. His coronation was succeeded by a sumptuous feast, at
which he regaled all the Swedish nobility. This
festival was contrived, like the kiss of Judas, to
veil the bloody scene that was soon to be enacted.
It was ended on the third day by the massacre of
ninety - four of the most distinguished noblemen
of Sweden, among whom was Erik, the father of
Gustavus Vasa. This nefarious crime, known in
history as the " Blood Bath," was concocted by
King Christian, the primate Trolle, and Deitrich
Slaghœk, the King's confessor, in order to get
rid of the nobility, who, by reason of their un-
bounded rights under the feudal system, were all-
powerful in the state. In order to preserve some
show of justice, Trolle proceeded against them
as *heretics*, having represented before the King
and people that the amnesty granted for crimes
against the State did not apply to crimes committed against the Church. As sovereign, he
might pardon his rebellious subjects, and was
bound by his promises to cast the mantle of

oblivion over their offences, but, as the minister
of St. Peter's successor on earth, he dare not refuse to execute the sentence pronounced against
them by God's Vicegerent on earth.   Accord-
ingly, after a mock trial, ninety-four ecclesiastics,
senators, knights, and burgomasters were pronounced guilty of heresy and schism, and delivered over to the secular power for execution.

On the 8th day of November, 1520, at dawn,
the gates of the city were closed ; loaded cannon
were planted in the great market-place ; guards
were stationed at the intersecting streets ; and the
death-like silence was broken by the tolling of
the castle-bell, and a long procession of the unfortunate, betrayed victims was marched forth to
their place of martyrdom.   They were all beheaded in the market-place, on a scaffold erected
in front of the King's palace.   They died in-
voking the vengeance of heaven on the perfidious
tyrant, his advisors, and perjured judges.   The
bodies of the victims lay in the market-place for
two days unburied, after which they were removed
and burned, together with the disinterred remains
of Sten Sture.   This was followed by the death
of many other prominent men throughout the

kingdom. As a matter of course, all Sweden
was filled with horror and alarm, and Christian
became the object of universal execration. History furnishes scarcely a page as dark as that of
the " Blood Bath."

Meanwhile, Gustavus Vasa, who seems to have
been consecrated by Providence to be the deliverer of Sweden, escaped from his confinement,
and, disguised as a peasant, wandered through
the country, and, having hired himself to a cattle
merchant, found his way to Lübeck in September, 1519, being pursued by Banner. The
people of Lübeck concluded it would not be
policy to increase the power of Christian, and
therefore granted hospitality to the illustrious
exile, and sent him in a merchant-vessel to his
native country in May, 1520. He arrived at
Calmar while it yet held out against the Danes ;
but the foreign mercenaries by whom it was
principally guarded, declined to receive a chief
of such desperate fortunes ; and, to escape be-
trayal into the hands of Christian, he withdrew
to Sudermania, where, in the disguise of a
peasant, he was concealed from his enemies.
During this time he came to the house of his

brother-in-law, Joachim Brake, penniless and
almost naked, just as the latter was preparing to
obey the summons of Christian to attend his
coronation. Brake would not be persuaded to
remain away from the ceremony, and, in conse-
quence, became one of the victims of the "Blood
Bath."

By royal proclamation, a price was now set on
the head of Gustavus Vasa, who was compelled
to skulk from one hiding-place to another, vainly
endeavoring to arouse his dejected countrymen
to resist the tyranny of their oppressors. The
castles of the great and the cottages of the poor
were alike shut against him. Even the monks
of the convent at Gripsholm, founded by his
ancestors, barred their gates on the friendless
and solitary wanderer. Under these discourag-
ing circumstances, he sought an asylum in the
remote and mountainous district of Dalecarlia,
where, deserted and robbed by his servant, he
was obliged to toil for his daily bread as a common workman in the copper-mines. The Dalecarlians were lovers of freedom, and, in their
wildness, always remained separate in dress and
manners from the other national tribes.

Gustavus, on account of his noble bearing and superior courage, soon became a favorite among them; and, having revealed himself to them, finally succeeded in arousing them to a sense of their country's wrongs. He reminded them of the heroic deeds of their fathers under Engelbrektson and the Stures — he admonished them of the frail tenure of their own possessions and lives under the tyranny of one who had so unjustly shed the noblest blood of Sweden. Roused by his enthusiasm and patriotism, they flew to arms, and fought for freedom. At their head he began his career as a general, and, under the favor and guidance of Providence, he finally drove the Danes out of Sweden. During the protracted struggle that followed, his valor, prudence, and abilities shone conspicuously, and endeared him more and more to his grateful countrymen. Success everywhere attended his efforts, until, finally, after acting as administrator during the war, he was chosen king. He established the Government on a firm basis, made the office of king hereditary instead of elective, and thus became the founder of that illustrious house that numbers among its descendants that irreproachable champion of Protestantism, Gustavus Adolphus. Thus terminated the Union of Calmar, after a nominal existence of one hundred and twenty-six years (1397–1523), which, during that time, proved a fruitful source of oppression to the Swedes, and of calamity to the whole northern people.

In order to form a proper estimate of the services of Gustavus Vasa, we must take a glance at the previous condition of society. The Government does not seem to have been firmly established, regularly defined, or uniformly administered. The affairs of state had hitherto been controlled chiefly by the clergy and the nobility. The high respect universally entertained for the clergy, afforded them an almost unlimited influence in public affairs; and superstition aided them with every facility for acquiring wealth. Commerce being either unknown or neglected, all the wealth of the kingdom consisted in the landed estates, and these were in the possession of the clergy and nobility, who even ceased gradually to pay their revenues to the crown. Fortifying their respective castles, they waged war upon each other, and the Government whenever they chose. The prelates and nobles com-

posed the Senate, and kept the power and wealth
of the country so completely in their own hands,
that the King could not, of his own accord, for-
tify a castle or maintain a guard of five hundred
men. The common people were serfs or slaves,
and the King no better than a captain-general in
time of war, and a nominal sovereign in time of
peace. The aristocracy, therefore, were equally
hostile to the people and the King, and were a
continual impediment in the way of the national
prosperity.

Such had been, for long years, the condition
of Sweden; and, from this unsettled and turbulent state of affairs, Gustavus Vasa, by his
courage, prudence, and statesmanship, was able
to frame a system of government which gave in-
ternal strength and stability to the nation, and
rendered it respectable and influential abroad.
The cruel massacre of the chief nobles by Christian II. relieved Gustavus of what might have
proved a serious difficulty in the regulation of
national affairs. To free himself from the op-
position of the Catholic clergy, — whose enmity,
under Trolle, he and his friends had so often
been forced to combat, — he established the Lu-

theran religion as the religion of the State, and
thus secured to the crown a considerable portion
of the landed estates of the kingdom. Not less
than thirteen thousand considerable properties
reverted to the crown, or were restored to their
original holders, and two-thirds of their revenues
were collected and put into the royal treasury.
He also caused the superfluous plate used in the
church services to be melted down and converted
into money for the use of the State. Some of the
prelates compounded by refunding their unpaid
taxes, which were applied to erecting and endow-
ing schools in time of peace, and the maintenance
of armies in time of war. He built roads and
bridges, and encouraged commerce and edu-
cation.

Such was the work Gustavus Vasa was called
upon to perform, and the manner in which he
discharged his duties gained for him the unlimited confidence of the people. They decreed
that his enemies should be the enemies of the
State; gave him power to declare war, levy taxes,
and do whatever he might think best for the
public good. From a rude, unlettered, turbulent Gothic aristocracy he formed a law-abiding

nation ; and, from this time, Sweden assumed a
place in the front rank of European govern-
ments in arts and arms, in letters and commerce.   From the house of Vasa sprang Gustavus
Adolphus and Charles XII.,-who, with the mem-
orable founder of the line, form a trio of the
most illustrious names in modern history.

Gustavus Vasa died September 7th, 1560, in
the 70th year of his age, having reigned thirty-
seven years.   He was buried in Upsala, the
ancient capital, the second place in dignity,
though not in size, and the seat of Sweden's
famous university.   There also lie interred the
remains of the celebrated chancellor Oxenstiern
and the immortal Linnæus, who was a native of
this place.

The services rendered Protestantism by Gustavus Vasa and his grandson, Gustavus Adolphus,
form one of the greatest themes of history.   The
latter ascended the throne in 1611, and, to the
time of his death at Lutzen, in 1632, was the
terror of his enemies.   He is almost the only
conqueror who did not, in the plenitude of his
power, forget God and moderation, and whose
strict sense of justice and integrity remained

uncorrupted by the glare of success and of riches. As Washington and Lincoln are to the people of the United States, so are Vasa and Adolphus to the people of Sweden.

In regard to Slaghœk, the instigator of the "Blood Bath," it may be proper to state that he ended his career by being put to torture and publicly burned in the market-place of Copenhagen. And Gustavus Trolle, after having vainly attempted to recover the liberty and crown of his master, Christian II., ended his turbulent and vindictive career in battle.

With regard to the fate of Christian II., history informs us that, failing in the subjugation of Sweden, and of oppressing his own people, a secret alliance was finally formed against him, accusing him of having misgoverned and oppressed the kingdom, and reduced the people to great misery. Hearing the news of this revolt, he fled ; and, to the astonishment of his subjects, instead of facing the storm, he equipped a small squadron, on board of which he embarked his family and most valuable effects, and sailed for the Low Countries. The Hollanders at Amsterdam subsequently furnished him vessels and

money to assist in the recovery of his domin-
ions, which resulted in the capture of Christian
and his confinement in the castle of Sonder-
borg, on a small island on the coast of Sleswig
(1533). There, incarcerated in a bastion of the
fort, the door walled up, with only one window,
and that looking over the sea, and a small hole
left on the other side for communication, with a
favorite dwarf as his only companion in this
dreary dungeon, King Christian II. expiated for
twelve long years the errors, vices, and crimes
of his earlier life. He was then removed in
1549 to the castle of Callundborg, on the west
coast of Jutland, where he had once confined
Gustavus Vasa, and he there underwent several
years more of lingering captivity. He died in
this castle in 1559, at the age of seventy-eight
years. During his confinement, his partisans
made several fruitless efforts to restore him to
his throne. Like many other bad men, he had
his friends; but his memory is execrated in history as "the Nero of the North," as "a Titus
in his laws and a Domitian in his actions."
*Though hand join in hand, the wicked shall not
be unpunished.*

On the other hand, Gustavus Vasa died amid the tears and praises of his people. No monarch was ever more universally esteemed or more sincerely regretted. His character was, indeed, extraordinary, considering the circumstances of the times in which he flourished. In an age of ignorance, he became learned; in a country the most barbarous, he organized a system of perfect civilization; among a nation of slaves, he restored public liberty; and, in the days of superstition and priestcraft, he set the consciences of men free from tyranny and spiritual thraldom. He seemed to be formed, in every respect, to excel the rest of mankind — uniting all the accomplishments that constitute the statesman, the warrior, the patriot, the hero, and the Christian. By his wise counsels and discreet policy, he raised the power and reputation of his Government to a height which rendered his name dear to his country and the admiration of all Europe. *When the righteous are in authority, the people rejoice; but when the wicked beareth rule, the people mourn. The king that faithfully judgeth the poor, his throne shall be established forever. Righteousness exalteth a nation, but sin is a reproach to any people.*

250

DALECARLIAN PEASANTS.

"The Dalecarlians are peculiar in their dress, which is now nearly what it was in the days of Gustavus Vasa. The male costume resembles somewhat that of English Quakers, and consists wholly of woollen cloth, of a black or white color, which creates a recognized distinction, and gives them the appearance of being sprung from a separate stock. The coat is wide in the sleeves, without collar or buttons, fastened down the breast with hooks and eyes. A low, broad-brimmed hat, a belt or cord tied round the waist, coarse gray stockings with red garters, huge wooden-soled shoes, with leather flap over the instep, complete the suit of this primitive race. The women are dressed in a little white cap fitting close to the face, a short woollen jacket, a brown or blue flannel skirt, an apron rudely embroidered, bright scarlet stockings, and wooden shoes with high heels coming almost under the centre of the foot." — *Crichton and Wheaton's History of* "*Denmark, Sweden, and Norway,*" published by Harper and Brothers, N. Y.

FALUN.

ALTHOUGH Sweden is not deficient in gold, silver, lead, and other ores, yet it is chiefly celebrated for its extensive and valuable copper and iron mines. The most famous copper-mine is in the ancient province of Dalecarlia, in the town of Falun, one hundred and twenty miles north-west of Stockholm. It is also called *Gamla Kopparberget*, the "Old Copper-Mine," because it has been worked for one thousand years. The mouth of the mine is a vast chasm, three-quarters of a mile in circumference, with a perpendicular depth of over one thousand feet. Some twelve hundred miners are employed in these extensive works. The copper is found in large masses. The greatest yield was in 1650, in which year three thousand tons were taken out. In 1690 it had declined to nineteen hundred tons; while the mine now yields only about four hundred tons.   Gustavus Adolphus used to call the mine the "treasury of Sweden."   The immense excavations extend for miles underground, and form vast chambers, in which Bernadotte, the late King of Sweden, gave splendid banquets, on which occasions the mines were brilliantly illuminated.   The prodigious number of smelting furnaces in the town send off their fumes into the air, so that its wooden houses present a blackened and gloomy appearance.   These fumes, though utterly destructive of all vegetable life in the neighborhood, it is said, do not affect the health of the people.   All kinds of absorbent food, however, are so much affected by the copper fumes that they taste bitter to one not accustomed to their use.

22

THE HANSA CITY OF LÜBECK.

LÜBECK is one of the free cities of northern Germany, and has existed since the eleventh century. In the twelfth century it received important privileges from the German emperors, which were retained even after it fell into the hands of the Danes, in 1201. In the year 1226 it was declared a free city, and has since maintained its independence. The population of the town is now about thirty-seven thousand, and that of the entire State is less than fifty thousand, of whom only three hundred are Roman Catholics—all the rest hold to the Lutheran Church. The town is noted for its specimens of Gothic architecture, its educational institutions, its provision for the poor, its laws, and its historical connection with the once famous and mighty Hanseatic League.

The Hansa was a Trades Union, organized in

the thirteenth century for the protection of the
trade of the cities of northern Europe.   Previous
to that time the merchants were exposed to the
rapacity of rulers, the lawless attacks of marauders
by land and of pirates by sea.   These trouble-
some enemies caused the formation of a league
or compact, called the Hansa; which name, in
the language of those Plattdeutsch traders, meant
a bond or compact for mutual aid.   The first
compact was entered into in 1219, between
Hamburg and two other cities, and was joined
by Lübeck in 1231, and by Brunswick in 1247.
The progress of the League was so rapid that in
1260 it held its first diet in Lübeck, and had then
already a regularly organized government and a
fixed system of finances and administration.   The
Hansa, at one time, numbered eighty-five towns,
and embraced every place of importance in
northern Germany.   It even established large
factories in London and other cities, and had
treaties of limited alliance with many distant
towns.

It attained high political influence — rulers
sought its favors and granted favors in return.
In order to promote its ends, it kept ships and

armed men. These armed forces frequently
came in conflict with the various political gov-
ernments. The greatest Powers thus came to
dread its hostility, and to seek its alliance;
though its professed object was simply to protect the commerce of its members by land and
sea, to extend that commerce among foreigners,
and, as far as possible, to exclude all competition
in trade. The Hansards exerted a wonderful influence in the expansion of commerce, agricul-
ture, and other industrial arts.

After being in existence two or three hundred
years, it began to lose its power, and, finally, was
nearly broken up in 1630. Three or four of the
cities, however, held to the compact even up to
the present century. Its decline was the result
of a great change in the circumstances which
originally gave it life, and made such an organi-
zation necessary. The highways on land and
sea were rendered safe for the transfer of goods
by the vigorous measures adopted by the various
Powers. The religious changes that had fer-
mented the heart of society had also much to
do with its extinction. Lübeck has a town-
house containing a library of fifty thousand

volumes, in which the archives of the famous Hanseatic League are still kept.

The principal motives which prompted Lübeck to assist the Swedes, under Gustavus Vasa, grew out of this Hansa and the Reformed religion, and were greatly intensified by past wars and subjection to the Danes.

INFLUENCE OF UNGUARDED REMARKS.

WHEN Rosanna told Bav that we "must ALWAYS obey the King," and when Gustavus Vasa, "in the bitterness of his heart," advised him to "become King Christian's executioner," they little dreamed what mighty consequences might follow their thoughtless words. Sportive, foolish, or unguarded advice given to children and simpletons has often led to most terrible and unexpected consequences. It is a thoughtless act, performed without the least intention of doing harm, and often by the best of people ; yet, lo! what sad deeds have been suggested in this very way. The following incident came under our personal notice : Two little boys once stood beside the carriage that was about to

convey their parents away from home, and inquired, "What shall we do while you are gone?"
The father sportively remarked, "Burn the hay-
stacks." What was his surprise and mortification, not to say pecuniary loss, on his return, to
find that the boys had literally carried out his
instructions. Let us ever be very careful what
advice and suggestions we make, and to whom
we give them.

ROSANNA'S ANSWER TO THE DANISH SOL-DIERY, DENYING ALL KNOWLEDGE AS TO THE WHEREABOUTS OF GUSTAVUS VASA.

Neither we nor the author would attempt to
excuse the falsehood told by Rosanna. * A lie
is a lie, whether spoken or acted that *good* may
come of it or not. God is strong enough to
help us, when our telling the truth seems to be to
the injury of a just cause. May we all have the
grace to tell the truth, and leave the conse-
quence to an overruling Providence.

* We do not pretend to make our characters perfect — an
error into which the writers of Sunday-school books are so
liable to fall.

THE END.